At last
father.

"But I was determined to keep the baby…
even if I had to raise him on my own!" Kate
touched her hand to her chest, as if to
calm her racing heart. "I wasn't expecting
you to support me even if I *did* manage
to contact you. I was wary of seeing you
again when we had only known each other
for a night."

Raising the child on her own… The thought
absolutely affronted his profound sense
of honor and his duty to do what was
right—not to mention the fact that this child
would be the sole heir to his family fortune
and all that Luca possessed! There was
no way—no way on God's earth—that Kate
was going to raise the baby alone!

MAGGIE COX loved to write almost as soon as she learned to read. Her favorite occupation was daydreaming and making up stories in her head, and this particular pastime has stayed with her through all the years of growing up, starting work, marrying and raising a family. No matter what was going on in her life—joy, happiness, struggle or disappointment—she'd go to bed each night and lose herself in her imagination. Through all the years of her secretarial career she kept filling exercise books and—joy oh joy—her word processor with her writing, never showing anyone what she wrote and basically keeping her stories for her own enjoyment. It wasn't until she met her second husband, the love of her life, that she was persuaded to start sharing those stories with a publisher. Maggie settled on Harlequin® Books, as she had loved romance novels since she was a teenager and read at least one or two paperbacks a week. After several rejections, the letters that were sent back from the publisher started to become more and more positive and encouraging, and in July 2002 she sold her first book, *A Passionate Protector,* to Harlequin Presents.

The fact that she is being published is truly a dream come true. However, each book she writes is still a journey in courage and hope, and a quest to learn and grow and be the best writer she can. Her advice to aspiring authors is "Don't give up at the first hurdle, or even the second, third or fourth, but keep on keeping on until your dream is realized. Because if you are truly passionate about writing and learning the craft, as Paulo Coelho states in his book *The Alchemist,* 'The Universe will conspire to help you' make it a reality."

PREGNANT WITH THE DE ROSSI HEIR

MAGGIE COX

~ THE ITALIAN'S BABY ~

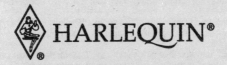

HARLEQUIN®

TORONTO • NEW YORK • LONDON
AMSTERDAM • PARIS • SYDNEY • HAMBURG
STOCKHOLM • ATHENS • TOKYO • MILAN • MADRID
PRAGUE • WARSAW • BUDAPEST • AUCKLAND

Recycling programs
for this product may
not exist in your area.

ISBN-13: 978-0-373-52760-1

PREGNANT WITH THE DE ROSSI HEIR

First North American Publication 2010.

Copyright © 2009 by Maggie Cox.

PREGNANT WITH THE
DE ROSSI HEIR

To Tony with all my love

CHAPTER ONE

'WELL, well, well… Look who it is!'

As the honeyed sea of that mesmerising voice reached her, washing around her ankles, threatening to pull her under, Kate Richardson stared in mute shock at the man facing her across the room. Her memory of his electric blue eyes having the power to dazzle like the most flawless glinting gemstones had not failed her, but she did not recall them having the ability to almost slice her in two even as he smiled. Uncurling her fingers from their death lock on the door handle, she knew her surprised expression must easily mirror his. But as she had barely any sensation of her facial muscles functioning at all Kate couldn't have sworn to it.

'Luca…' All she could do right then was stare in wonder, because her mental faculties seemed frighteningly slow in catching up with her speech.

'At least you remember my name.'

Did he really think she would ever forget it? 'The agency sent me.' Kate could barely find the words to explain her presence. 'You—you need a secretary for the next few days…apparently.' Her shoulders lifted in a nervous shrug.

His jaw hardened. No spare flesh spoilt its perfect symmetry—it was just jutting, formidable bone. '*Dio!* I know perfectly well what I need! Come in and close the door!'

Kate obeyed, unable to disregard his harsh-voiced command even if she'd wanted to. Inhabiting the same electrically charged space as this man was like being swept along by a powerful current she couldn't fight, and for a moment the sensation of vulnerability this instigated was too real to combat. She'd had no idea he worked in London… *none.* But then what she *did* know about the provoking specimen of masculinity glaring at her from across the room she could probably commit to just a single sentence. In the breathtaking few hours they had spent together in Milan three months ago, they hadn't exactly immersed themselves in personal biographies. They had been held in thrall by other, far more distracting discoveries about each other instead.

'Sit down.'

His authoritative command ricocheted through the tensely strung atmosphere like a velvet gunshot. Swallowing hard, Kate pulled out the chair on the opposite side of the huge modern desk and sat. *She was glad to.* Her legs were suddenly about as substantial as flimsy threads of cotton.

The huge plate-glass window behind her interrogator reflected a stunning vista that included Big Ben and the London Eye, but the imposing landmarks didn't distract her. How could they when they were in unfair competition with the artfully sculpted male visage before her? Kate's heart soared and her insides fluttered as she recalled that she knew intimately that his incredible body was equally as artfully designed. *And there had been an altogether shocking and unexpected price to pay for that intimate knowledge,* she reflected soberly, and her stomach executed an unsettling cartwheel at the fact.

'Why did you leave without saying goodbye in Milan? Do you usually treat your lovers so casually? Leaving them in the morning without so much as the good manners to at least wait until they are awake? Do you get some kind of strange satisfaction out of such behaviour?'

Dumbstruck, Kate stared, feeling her cheeks burn in indignation and shock. 'I beg your pardon?'

'Last time we met your hearing was not impaired in any way, as far as I can recall.' His disdain was clearly intended to sting.

'I'm just a little taken aback that you would believe I do that sort of thing regularly. Let me assure you that I don't!'

'The fact of the matter is that you did it to *me*, Katherine… For some reason I expected better from you…but you disappointed me.'

Powerful regret washed over Kate. If she could have had that time back again would she act differently? *Maybe.* Hindsight was a wonderful thing.

Studying the handsome, disapproving face before her, Kate knew a sudden great desire to have him smile at her. So consuming was it that she could almost have wept in frustration, knowing that her wish was in vain. An icy chill shuddered through her. Thinking back to the party at some big-wig architect's mansion that her friend Melissa had dragged her to, courtesy of the swish property developer she worked for, Kate had considered it a mistake right from the off. It had been the last evening of her holiday, and all she had really wanted to do was spend time in quiet reflection on how she was going to rebuild her life when she got back to the UK.

How did a person learn to trust again when they had been betrayed as brutally as Kate had?

Her plans had been hijacked by her friend's insistence that she needed to 'get out and have some fun,' and instead of the quiet evening she'd had in mind she had had to endure the uncomfortable proximity of a bunch of strangers in a glamorous setting that had no power to lift her out of the despondency she'd been in. That was until the man now in front of her had appeared, cast his eyes round the room as though already bored with the faces that glanced back at him, and then shockingly rested his far too disturbing gaze on *her*.

Mel had been off hobnobbing somewhere else, and Kate had sensed her legs turn as weak as a newborn foal's beneath the charismatic stranger's sizzling observation. He had turned his back on several guests clearly eager to speak to him to cross the room and talk to her instead, introducing himself as 'Luca,' she recalled. *Just Luca*. There had been no mention of Gianluca De Rossi. And Kate had offered her name as Katherine. It was her full name, but she rarely used it, so why it had slipped out so naturally beneath his unsettling gaze was a mystery.

Except that maybe a person couldn't be expected to be totally in control of their responses when they were confronted by an aura of wealth, confidence and breathtaking good looks such as Luca was so commandingly in possession of? And maybe at that moment she had also succumbed to feeling small and insecure, and had needed the bolster of a name that sounded a bit classier than just plain Kate?

There were many reasons she'd acted so out of character that unforgettable night, and that was just the first of them... Clasping her hands in front of her now, on the polished surface of the desk, it took every bit of courage she could muster to meet the disapproving gaze Luca was still directing her way and hold it.

'I hadn't *planned* to leave the way I did. I just...I just didn't want to wake you. It was the last night of my holiday and I had a plane to catch. I should have mentioned it before, but—' She blushed, certain her cheeks were glowing red as ripe russet apples.

'But we were otherwise engaged at the time?' Luca suggested wryly, a visible muscle throbbing at the side of his fascinating cheekbone. 'Even so...you should have woken me—not just left without so much as leaving a phone number or an address where I could contact you!'

'I'm sorry.' Kate meant it, and there was a

helpless catch in her voice. Yet part of her was reeling at the idea that a man who moved in the privileged and exclusive circles Luca did even *cared* that his one-night lover had not left a number or address where he might reach her. *Was she wrong to have assumed he would forget her so easily?* Had she just convinced herself of that so that she could get over the pain of leaving him and never seeing him again by making the cut quick and clean? Because it *had* pained her to leave him…

The attraction that had flared between them had smoked white-hot the second their glances had met, and even Kate's relative inexperience with men hadn't fooled her into thinking that was a common, everyday thing. And underlying that blistering magnetic pull she'd miraculously sensed the kind of soul-to-soul connection she'd long dreamed of. There had definitely been something special about Luca that Kate had not been able to forget. But at the time she'd been grieving on two counts. Grieving for the loss of her mother as well as for the loss of her fiercely guarded self-esteem—brought about by the *other* thing that had so devastatingly occurred back home. Both those momentous events had left Kate in no fit state either to think straight *or* make good decisions. And now she had to contend with the unbelievable twist of fate that had brought her right back into this man's charismatic sphere again—turning up for a temp assignment that meant she would be his personal assistant for the next couple of weeks, while his permanent PA was on holiday.

'Well…on reflection, I think it probably best that we simply forget what has happened between us in the past and concentrate on the present. It is unfortunate that this has come about, but we will just have to live with it if we are to work together over the next two weeks.'

Luca sighed, as if weighed down with too much responsibility. Beneath the fluid expensive weave of his faultless Italian tailoring, his hard lean body emitted a palpable sense of weariness, and Kate got the definite impression that work had been driving him to the exclusion of all else lately. It made her want to alleviate the burden for him somehow.

'Though I have to say,' he continued, 'it is a very strange coincidence indeed that you should turn up in my office to stand in as my secretary, is it not? Tell me the truth, Katherine. Has someone put you up to this as some kind of joke? Tell me now, before I have to take the regrettable step of calling Security and getting them to escort you out of the building!'

She gasped. 'What are you saying? Of course it's not a joke! The agency I work for sent me and that's the absolute truth! I had no idea that Gianluca De Rossi was you! How could I? You never told me your full name that night, and neither did you tell me you worked in London! I naturally assumed you worked in Milan.'

'But you could have asked anyone at the party my full name and they would have enlightened you. It was my house and *my* party, after all! It would have been easy if you had probed further to discover that I have an office in London as well as Milan, and that I am mainly based here.'

'For your information, apart from the friend I went with I spoke to hardly anyone else that entire evening but you! And my friend didn't know who you were. She was given the invitation by someone in her office who couldn't go, and her only information was the address! Anyway, why would I wait three months if I wanted to see you again? If I'd wanted to stay in touch it would have been far easier to leave you my details back in Milan!'

'So you are telling me that you purposely did *not* want to get in touch? How flattering!' Luca's mouth pursed, as though he had tasted something disagreeable. 'And now—if I am to believe what you say is true—it is fate that has conspired to bring us together again! I suppose one could conclude from that that we must have some unfinished business after all. What do you think, Katherine?'

Suddenly feeling quite faint, Kate frowned. *What did he mean, exactly?* She was doubly perturbed by his words when she considered the potentially explosive secret she was keeping that he didn't yet know about… She just about held on to her scant breakfast of dry toast when she thought about that.

'Unfinished business or not, I'm here to work as your secretary, and genuinely that's the only reason I'm here!'

'Then if you are to work for me, know this! I expect you to be absolutely first-class at what you do. I will not be looking upon you with any leniency because of what happened between us before! Are you up to the task, Katherine? Because if you are not then I will ring the agency now and get them to send somebody else.'

His smile was laced with mistrust as well as a deep cynicism. It wasn't at all like the one Kate had been acquainted with, that had lit up a room as brightly as a hundred-watt lightbulb. Her stomach churned with misery and shock.

'You don't need to get anyone else. I'm good at what I do and completely professional!'

'Well, then,' Luca continued, 'as long as you know that I am hardly accustomed to women treating me as an opportunity for some kind of casual sexual release, and that there will be no chance of a repeat performance, our working together should perhaps not pose too many problems after all.'

'It wasn't like that! I never—'

'You never *what*, Katherine? You never had a one-night stand before, or you never left a man's bed the morning after without saying goodbye? How do I know what is the truth? I only have the evidence of my own regrettable experience to go on as far as you are concerned, and the fact is that you *did* leave the next morning with clearly no intention of ever getting in touch with me again!'

'It wasn't like that at all! And it was never my intention to treat you as some kind of casual sexual release, I assure you! There were reasons why I left the way I did.'

'A plane to catch, you said?'

'Not just that.' Feeling as if she was on a rock face, scrabbling for purchase, Kate gave Luca a nervous smile in the hope that she might somehow get through to him. After all, hadn't they shared something special that momentous night, when they had not been able to ignore the passion and urgency that had driven them into each other's arms? Something that had fuelled Kate's sense of something vital having been missing in her life as nothing else had ever done before?

But it took only an instant for her to realise that whatever faint hope she'd nurtured for Luca's understanding was a waste of time. The look on his face already told her that sympathy from him was in frighteningly short supply.

'Something had happened at home that I was desperately trying to deal with at the time,' she started to explain, agitatedly linking and unlinking her hands together. 'That's why I'd gone to Italy…to try and sort myself out. I know you might find this hard to believe, but the way I behaved that night was so out of character that the following morning…waking up in your bed…I was— I couldn't believe I had— I mean—'

'It sounds like you are making excuses up as you go—and not even very good ones at that!'

Frustrated at her woeful inability to try and explain, and with her stomach cramping in distress, Kate shrugged disconsolately. 'You're obviously not going to forgive me, so perhaps it *is* best if you just ring the agency and get them to send somebody else in my place?'

'No. I will give you one chance. What I propose to do is give you a one-day trial, and if you do not measure up to the high standards I expect *then* I will contact the agency for a replacement!'

'I suppose I can't argue with that.'

Even if she didn't like the idea of failing Luca's one-day trial, Kate breathed a silent prayer of thanks that he was at least going to give her a chance to prove herself, and not simply show her the door as she'd increasingly been expecting him to.

'Now…I have already wasted enough time this morning and I must get on! We have a busy day ahead, and there are several things on the agenda that must be done. With your assistance I will try to accomplish as much as possible before I have to go to an important appointment at the Dorchester Hotel with a Saudi Arabian client who is also a good friend of mine. He is only in London for two days, and tonight I am throwing a small party for him and some colleagues he wants me to meet. In the meantime you can familiarise yourself with the notes my PA left for you. Her office is just through that door there, and unless I particularly have the need to be private the door between us stays *open*. Knowing your disconcerting habit for leaving without warning, Katherine, I think that is a sensible precaution under the circumstances—do you not agree?'

Staring at him, and realising that he clearly had very little respect for her because she'd left him the way she had that morning without explanation, Kate knew that she could not make matters even worse by walking out now. Something had happened between them that night they'd spent together in Italy—something that had had dramatic and far-reaching consequences—and Kate *owed* it to Luca to reveal it to him now that she'd been given the chance. No matter what his reaction to her news, there was simply no way she could or would duck out of telling him the truth. No matter how difficult the telling might be.

'If that's the way you want it, then that's fine with me!' Pushing to her feet and finding that her legs were still as insubstantial as tissue paper, Kate made her way towards the door Luca had indicated, into the office that would possibly be hers for the next fortnight. As she passed him, he struck out his hand and caught her by the elbow.

'What?' Her glance was alarmed.

For a moment the glittering intensity of his cerulean blue eyes seem to arrow right down into her soul, and the heat from his hand burned through her clothing, almost sapping her will and her strength with its power to unravel her.

'*Niente*…nothing!'

He dropped her arm as though touching it somehow contaminated him and, feeling her stomach plummet like a stone, Kate moved through the opened door and into the stylish, perfectly neat office on the other side.

Driving his hands deep into his trouser pockets, Luca found he needed several moments to compose himself after the volatile encounter with the woman that it had been so hard for him to forget. *Madre mia!* He had thought he was seeing a ghost when she'd walked into his office! Such had been the dreamlike quality of their scorching but brief encounter in Milan that he could surely be forgiven for starting to believe he had conjured her up from his too-fevered imagination? Even now his heartbeat had still not resumed its regular normal cadence after he had seen her. His nostrils twitched at the evocative scent that lingered in her wake after he'd angrily let go of her arm. It called to mind a rain-washed English country garden, and was more provocative than any other sultry perfume he had ever encountered.

As if to echo his heated thoughts, a forceful, primal longing registered deep in his belly, and Luca pulled out the sumptuous leather chair behind his desk and dropped down into it, tunnelling his fingers with frustration through his thick, dark hair. Even his usually highly reliable photographic memory had not done Katherine justice, he concluded. She was even *more* bewitching than he recalled, with that soft mane of waving sable hair that no style could or should try to tame, and those glistening raven-dark eyes with their lustrous lashes that even the most artful make-up could not hope to enhance—for how did one enhance perfection? But along with her eyes and her alluring sexy body it was the memory of her passionate, sweetly giving mouth that had the power to keep Luca awake nights. Just one glance at close quarters—as he had experienced just now—was enough to make him want to crush it ravenously beneath his own and once again sample its ripe strawberry and vanilla sweetness with abandon.

Dio! What was he going to do now? Was he crazy even to entertain the idea of allowing Katherine to be his secretary for the next two weeks, given that his body still clearly desired her? And in spite of her casual treatment of their night together? *Probably.*

But then he could be equally casual if he chose. He was certainly not looking for any kind of deep and meaningful relationship with the woman, so what had he to fear?

Sighing heavily, Luca recalled that night three months ago in Milan. There had been something about Katherine that had provoked the strongest reaction in him—and surprisingly it wasn't all about sex. No…he had intuited an innate *goodness* about her that had made all his friends appear worryingly shallow in comparison. A man did not brush up against such innocence and goodness often, but when he did he never forgot it. Although right now Luca honestly could not attest to whether fate was on his side or not, delivering Katherine to his door as it apparently had. There was still her inexplicable departure the next morning to contend with, as well as the blow to his pride at hearing that she had not particularly *wanted* to get in touch with him again. Apart from his inconvenient desire, Luca was still too sceptical to believe unquestioningly that destiny was doing him a favour.

After losing Sophia three years ago in such a bitter and tragic way, he had all but relinquished any hope for future happiness anyway. When Katherine had left him that morning in Milan, after his initial confusion and frustration Luca had told himself to just put it down to experience and forget her. If he had wanted to locate her he could easily have asked friends at the party—the friends he had practically ignored all evening because he'd been so enthralled by her—for more information to help track her down. But at the time Luca had determinedly resisted the impulse. That night of the party he had found something of his wife's that had stirred up some painful memories, and no doubt that was what had driven him into the arms of a woman he barely knew. Usually he was much more circumspect, and took time to get to know a woman before he took her to bed. *It had certainly taught him a valuable lesson about the consequences of giving way to pure lust and emotion!*

Once again Luca drove his restless hands through his tousled dark hair and shook his head at his re-membered experience of a regrettable loss of control. Whatever reason Katherine had for showing up to work as his PA, from now on he would defi-nitely be judging her on her professional acumen and *not* his attraction for her, he vowed!

CHAPTER TWO

THE door between her boss's office and hers remained ominously open, and Kate deliberately didn't glance towards it as often as her sometimes racing heart dictated. Even though—perversely, perhaps—she longed for a glimpse of the man occupying the adjoining room. The man who barked out instructions as though he cared little how she received them, and who clearly intended to treat her like someone well beneath him on the social strata while she was working for him.

She might well have despaired when she recalled the warmth Luca had exhibited towards her the night they had made love, but Kate refused to do so. Feeling sorry for herself would get her nowhere. *But her already delicate stomach had churned many times that morning when she thought in distress about the secret she kept. A secret that she now*

likened to carrying smuggled contraband through
a highly volatile airport Customs on red alert after
the less than overjoyed way Luca had reacted to
seeing her again.

That magical night in Milan seemed like the
most incredible dreamlike fantasy when she considered the mistrustful and disapproving air he was
treating her with now. And if he were already sus-
picious of her motives for being there, what would
he be like when he heard the astounding news she
was waiting to reveal?

The revelation was something Kate had wanted
to tell him about, but she had not been able to
because she had simply had no way of contacting
him. After getting a job in the States, her friend
Melissa had unexpectedly left Italy, and had not yet
contacted Kate with her new address or phone
number. And she had been unable to recall the full
address of the mansion where the party had been
that night—let alone the place of work where
Melissa had been employed! All avenues leading to
contact with Luca had been closed to her, it seemed,
and Kate had told herself time and time again that
it was her own stupid fault for not leaving him a way
to contact *her*.

Back in the present, she forced herself to deal

with the tasks in front of her and knew she would have to bide her time as far as choosing the right moment to break her news to Luca. The thing was, apart from anything else, she really *needed* this job and had no intention of failing his little 'trial'. The agency was paying her the top rate for this particular assignment, and the extra money would definitely come in handy given the situation that faced her. In fact that was an understatement. She'd been trying to save as much as she could, but living in London was expensive, and the amount she had squirrelled away so far would hardly help her exist for a month without a job, let alone for the foreseeable future! The dilemma had already given Kate many sleepless nights.

Putting her worries aside, it didn't take her long to find her usual professional stride, yet there was no let-up as far as her stomach was concerned. Her insides continued to turn over like some demented Ferris wheel, not letting her forget for even a second that she was effectively living with a ticking bomb until she spoke to Luca.

'Come into my office, would you?'

Luca didn't wait for Kate to rise from her desk. After briefly putting his head round the door he immediately returned to his room. The plush domain, with its modern, state-of-the-art furniture and its tastefully framed prints of grand public buildings and luxurious homes clearly designed for a fabulously wealthy clientele, proudly reflected his firm's impressive architectural achievements and the fact that they were amongst the top echelon of the experts in their field. Lucy—the employment agency manager—had been eager to point out how incredibly successful the De Rossi empire was when she had outlined the details of the job to Kate.

Quickly collecting her notepad and pen, Kate was conscious of not wanting to keep her boss waiting.

'Sit down,' he commanded without preamble.

It was hard to maintain a purely professional focus when the cologne Luca wore so potently underlined his devastating appeal. Little tingles of highly erotic awareness sizzled up and down Kate's spine as she detected musky notes of sandalwood and amber. The scent was a stunning and provocative reminder of the sensual, beautiful night they'd spent together and how amazing he had been as a lover. Everything about the man had enthralled Kate. From the expensive way he smelled to his rich, lightly accented voice, and the way every silk-skinned, taut and toned muscle in his incredible body had flexed so unforgettably beneath her awed fingers.

Because she feared he might somehow guess what was in her mind, she could hardly bring herself to meet the disturbing blue gaze that seemed to have no such hesitation in frankly appraising *her*.

'My friend Hassan has been in touch with me, and I am just about to leave to go to our meeting. I am glad to see that you are wearing a formal jacket over your dress and that the length of the garment is a respectable one, because I need you to accompany me,' Luca remarked, turning the gold fountain pen he held between his fingers over and over again, as though too much restless energy was pouring through his veins to be easily contained. 'Although Hassan is quite a westernised Saudi, first impressions are everything, and I need my PA to reflect the professionalism and cordiality we absolutely pride ourselves on in this firm.'

Indignant heat flooded into Kate's cheeks that Luca obviously felt the need to emphasise points she naturally took as read—and with a look that seemed close to disparaging. 'I'm not unfamiliar with Saudi culture!' she replied heatedly. 'I once worked for an oil company in Dubai for six months, so I do know what is expected! Apart from that, I naturally know how to conduct myself in a professional manner when it comes to dealing with my boss's clients. I would not have lasted this long as a personal assistant if I didn't!'

A dark eyebrow quirked skywards in the sardonic face at the other side of the desk. 'You are full of surprises, Katherine. I see that I cannot take anything for granted where you are concerned. But I know that to my cost already…do I not?'

'Was there anything else?' Deliberately biting her lip on a retort, Kate desperately renewed her silent mantra to keep calm and not lose her cool. Although Luca might take perverse pleasure in baiting her, apparently believing her to be deserving of nothing but his scorn, she wouldn't add to the already simmering tension between them by rising to it. There was still the most important topic of all to discuss, and it hovered over her like an avalanche poised to do its devastating worst. Sooner or later Kate was going to have to call upon even deeper emotional reserves and just say it.

'Yes. You might want to freshen your make-up a little and tie your hair back before we leave. I would not want that unruly mane of silk to prove distracting to my client and friend when we are in the throes of discussing important business!'

Kate stared at Luca in disbelief. He made it sound as though she was deliberately wearing her hair loose to provoke and allure! She was aware by now that he would probably take every opportunity he could over the next two weeks to belittle and mock her in any way that presented itself to his richly creative imagination, but descending to personal levels of criticism was a step too far in Kate's book. Okay, her hair *did* have a tendency to defy any attempt to control its unruly wave, but she always kept it at a manageable shoulder length and made sure it was clean, shiny and healthy!

Unfortunately, his reference had provoked an unhappy childhood memory in Kate. Sometimes less than kind classmates in the grammar school she had attended had taunted her as a 'scruffy little gypsy'. Just because she'd lived in a council flat and not in one of the wide leafy avenues where many of their own more affluent homes had been situated! It was fair to say a sense of not being good enough had definitely dogged Kate throughout her life because of her negative experience at school, but no way would she let this privileged, arrogant man relegate her to that insecure intimidated child again just because he held a grudge against her!

Gripping her notepad hard between her fingers, Kate sat up even straighter in her chair, anger over-taking the hurt that still lingered in her mind. 'I really don't appreciate such personal comments about my hair! And, for however short or long I work for you, you had better keep your thoughts on my appearance to yourself! For your information I've been a PA for nearly eight years, and in all that time I've never had one word of complaint about the way I wear my hair or how I look!'

'I do not doubt it! But then I suspect that most of your bosses have been men, have they not?'

'What exactly are you implying?'

'You do not need me to spell it out for you, do you Katherine?' Shifting in the luxurious leather chair so that it creaked with the movement, Luca leant forward and pierced her with the unsettling vivid glare of his sky-blue eyes. 'Of *course* no healthy heterosexual male with hot red blood in his veins would voice a complaint about how you look! Privately they might find it somewhat of a challenge to have a girl with such—shall we say—*distracting* assets around. But I'm sure you realise I mean that in a complimentary way, and not as an insult.'

She didn't want his compliments… Not when they were edged with such obvious underlying resentment towards her. Kate swallowed hard.

'So. When are we leaving?' Pushing to her feet, she was surprised when Luca followed suit. Again she felt at a disadvantage next to his imposing height, as well as from being the recipient of an arrogant glance that was surely meant to make her feel even smaller!

'My car will be out front in ten minutes' time,' he told her, his flawless diamond gaze travelling almost insolently up and down her body.

She was wearing the smartest dress and jacket she possessed. Of course he would immediately see they were not of the same quality of his own expensive attire, Kate realised, but his glance was disturbing for another reason. Smart clothes were little protection from the inescapable idea that Luca's knowledge of her body was already the most intimate possible, and her sense of vulnerability in his company increased uncomfortably.

Feeling heat prickle at the back of her neck and in the sensitive tips of her breasts, she self-consciously drew the edges of her jacket together, as if the neckline of her dress was too revealing. *It wasn't*.

'I'd better go and get ready, then.'

Just as she reached the door, Luca addressed her again. 'Leave your hair. I have changed my mind about it. Do not trouble yourself tying it back. I will collect the necessary architectural plans and see you outside by the car.'

And with that he picked up the telephone receiver and snapped out an impatient order to the poor, unsuspecting receptionist at the desk on the ground floor…

Luca paused for a moment in mid-discussion of plans for a new, spectacularly modern hotel his friend Hassan was having built in his home city of Dubai. Although Luca was responsible for the initial design, there were two senior colleagues who had been with him in the original discussions who would be overseeing the build in the city itself. Right now they were both out of the country until the weekend, so naturally Hassan wanted to deal with the chief architect and his friend—Luca himself.

Luca had momentarily paused in what he was saying because the older man was none too discreetly staring at the woman who sat at the far end of the triangle of sumptuous armchairs in the floral-scented meeting room, taking notes. Observing the other man's undoubted interest, Luca was unprepared for the scalding burn of jealousy that made the muscularly lean wall of his taut stomach harden like steel. *Not that he could blame what he knew to be his friend's notorious roving eye for alighting with such blatant speculation on Katherine.* For just over three interminable months Luca had alternately been taunted and frustrated by the memory of her exquisite beauty, and had privately acknowledged that there had been something about her other than just an unforgettable face that made all men long to know her and possess her. *But he had not allowed himself to speculate too deeply on the subject.* All he knew right now was that no other woman could beguile so emphatically simply by wearing a shop-bought dress and jacket, the minimum of make-up and with no evidence of jewellery of any kind adorning her.

The admission did not help improve his mood. Frustration had been building in him ever since Katherine had walked into his office, and although his desire seemed to be acting independently of his will he was wary of being made a fool of by her a second time. He cleared his throat and Hassan glanced back at him, completely at ease and not at all abashed at being caught out ogling Luca's PA.

'You were saying, Luca?' He smiled.

Briefly catching Katherine's eye in silent rebuke, as if it were all *her* fault that the other man was so frankly appraising her, Luca seamlessly resumed from where he had left off. But he had to seriously tamp down an almost irresistible urge to wish the meeting at an end so he could whisk her back to the office, where he could at least be alone with her again.

Knowing he was feeling both predatory and possessive, he should have despised himself for a weakness that could only bring him more of the bitter pain he had been living with for too long— but his ego urged Luca not to let Katherine run out on him a second time before exacting some kind of payment in kind from her for her unexpected desertion that morning....

An hour later, the meeting at an end and Luca's friend's concerns and questions about the proposed new hotel satisfactorily appeased, the wealthy Arab took the younger man aside in the elegant lobby of the hotel. 'Luca...I have to ask. Your secretary...she is a single woman?' He glanced over at Katherine, standing patiently near the exit, waiting for Luca to finish his business and join her. 'I observed no wedding ring on her finger.'

For a stricken moment the most unwelcome thought of all shook Luca out of any semblance of equilibrium left to him. He had considered it before, of course, and now he was forced to consider it again. What if Katherine was married, and *that* was why she had left him without explanation in Milan, leaving no way for him to contact her? *Had she regretted her adultery with him and, overwhelmed with guilt, fled before he could discover any personal details with which to incriminate her?* He sensed himself frown deeply, felt his stomach tied in knots.

'No,' he said clearly, hoping fervently it was the truth. 'She is not married.'

'Then is there a man in her life? Someone serious, I mean?'

Feeling the twisting knots in his insides lock tighter, Luca kept his expression as impassive as he was able. 'I am not aware that Katherine is seeing anyone else, my friend, but I can tell you that she and I *do* have some unfinished business shall we say? Does that answer your question?'

The Arab's large coal-black eyes widened in surprise. Beneath his elegant designer suit he shrugged his massive shoulders and grinned. 'I can see you are indeed the dark horse, my friend! But then your interest in her does not surprise me! Who could blame you for taking advantage of the chance to be with such innocent loveliness?'

In unison, both men moved their gaze to where Katherine still stood. Her slender yet shapely figure in her navy blue polka-dot dress, her beautiful eyes and dark gleaming hair were drawing other admiring glances besides their own, Luca observed with another helpless flash of jealousy.

'I would give much to experience just one night with such a woman!' Hassan slapped Luca heartily on the back. 'No offence intended, my friend,' he added quickly, seeing that the Italian's mouth had firmed in what was clearly disapproval. 'You are a lucky, lucky man!'

That was a matter of opinion, Luca thought in bittersweet reflection, glancing across at Katherine.

'That aside,' Hassan continued cheerfully, 'I look forward to seeing you tonight at the little party you have most kindly arranged at your house for me and my business associates from Riyadh. They are most keen to talk to you about the incredible work you do, and if I am not mistaken, and things go well, you will no doubt have another valuable commission by the end of the evening!'

Unable to ignore the pangs of hunger that gripped her for another minute, and having forgotten to pack the dry biscuits she'd grown accustomed to carrying with her of late, Kate knocked lightly on the opened door between her office and Luca's to get his attention.

'What is it?'

His less than friendly response might have been

intimidating if Kate wasn't already getting used to it. Stepping inside the larger room, she saw that he was poring over some architectural drawings on the huge desk in front of him. The knot of his dark silk tie had been pulled a good three inches away from his pristine white shirt collar, and the tousled appearance of his thick dark hair also suggested that the work he faced was perhaps momentarily getting the better of him. *The man worked like a Trojan*, Kate observed. It was half past two in the afternoon and she'd seen no indication of him being even *close* to stopping for lunch or even a cup of coffee.

She frowned. 'I wonder if I could pop out to get myself a sandwich? I didn't eat breakfast this morning, and I don't know about you, but I'm feeling rather hungry. Perhaps I could get you something too?'

He stared at her...really *stared*. As the silence in the room became almost deafening, Kate's feet seemed rooted to the floor by his disconcerting examination.

'Did you hear what I said?' she asked, her throat tightening with tension.

'My friend Hassan asked me if you were married,' Luca drawled, his blue eyes once again travelling slowly and deliberately up and down her body.

Kate's hunger pangs were instantly demolished.

Instead, hunger of a very different kind clawed at her. His lascivious glance made her feel as if he was physically touching her, and it made her shiver with want. But then the full import of his question finally found its way to central control in her brain, and a sense of deep shock rippled through her.

'*Are* you married, Katherine?' Luca asked.

'No! I'm not! And why should that be any concern of your client's?'

'You must have seen how he looked at you?'

'I was busy taking the notes of the meeting!'

'Anyway…it is not my friend's interest in the answer that I am concerned with. It is my own. So, if you are not married, what about a boyfriend?'

'I have none! Is that what you thought? That I was two-timing someone when I was with you?'

'It did occur to me, not long after I woke up and found you gone, that perhaps too much champagne the night before at the party had made you—possibly a married woman—a little reckless, shall we say? That maybe you were just looking for a good time and when opportunity knocked…you took it. In the morning, discovering what you had done, you were perhaps overcome by guilt and regret and decided to flee before you incriminated yourself further…'

'Well, you're wrong! It was nothing like that at all!'

Feeling distressed at the idea that Luca had even considered that she had run out on him because she was married or involved with someone else, Kate crossed her bare arms over the silk bodice of her dress and despairingly tried to straighten her thoughts. *How could he think such a thing?* she asked herself. Had she imagined the bond they had shared? A bond that she'd firmly believed had transcended the merely physical?

'Then how *was* it, Katherine? And this time perhaps you will do me the courtesy of telling me the truth of why you ran out on me that morning?'

The truth. How simple that sounded… And yet the reality was that it wasn't simple at all. It was a terrible, never to be repeated, embarrassing…*mess*.

CHAPTER THREE

UP UNTIL just over six months earlier, Kate had been engaged to be married to Hayden Michaels, a successful, handsome broker she'd met at a temp job she'd been doing in the City. A 'wunderkind' of the company, he was a young man with great ambition who worked hard to get what he wanted but played hard too.

Kate hadn't been bowled over by him at the start. On the contrary, her cautious nature had warned her against getting involved with a man who seemed to treat life as one big party and one huge opportunity to plunder the honey-pot for all it was worth. She'd been taught firm, solid values by her mother, who had raised her single-handedly, and Kate's own secret, small ambition was that one day she would meet the man of her dreams, fall in love and have the family that she longed for. As an only child she had yearned for brothers and sisters, and had often felt lonely growing up. *Being bullied at school hadn't helped her sense of alienation.* She'd always been only too aware of the struggle her mother had had to make ends meet, and so instead of going on to university when she'd got her A level results, she had opted to go to secretarial college for a year, get some qualifications, then go out to work to help alleviate some of her mother's financial burdens.

Over the years she'd dated on and off, but had never found the partner she'd secretly been hoping for. When she'd met the handsome and fun-loving Hayden Michaels something about him had appealed to Kate, but she'd known instinctively he wasn't the type of man who would want to settle down with a wife and family. *Not whilst ambition was his driving force.* She had decided to resist his appeal. Yet day after day, week after week, as Kate had worked alongside him in the office, his bold smile, perpetual good humour and unflagging determination to get her to go out with him had finally persuaded her to give him a chance. Her mother had passed away suddenly from a heart attack just two months before she'd met him, and Kate had been *lonely.* Even if mother and daughter had not shared the closest of relationships... As time had gone by she'd begun to see another side to her new boy-friend…a side that had warmed her heart much more than the expensive gifts, designer clothes and meals at Michelin-starred restaurants he'd insisted on treating her to. It had been a sensitive, perhaps vulnerable side, that had hinted at his fear of failure, of being judged not good enough by his peers and friends, of not being able to sustain any success he had achieved. Perhaps Kate's ever-alert antennae had picked up on the very things that she herself had struggled with since those days at school when she had been taunted for being the poor girl in the class. The one whose mother hadn't been able to afford to take her on foreign holidays or buy her trendy clothes and expensive dance classes like the other girls' parents had.

Truth to tell, it hadn't been the lack of all those things that had left Kate so vulnerable. No. It had been the lack of demonstrable affection from her only parent that had got to her the most. Worn out with working too hard and worrying how to make ends meet, Liz Richardson had grown a hard shell around her heart that had kept her daughter from getting anywhere near her emotionally. But coupled with a legacy of childhood bullying and the sense of low self-esteem that she had perhaps naturally inherited from such an upbringing, Kate had found her own heart becoming guarded and wary. Even when men had told her they found her attractive, there had always been a part of her that never quite believed them, secretly waiting to hear the truth. That she was *none* of those desirable things they said she was, that she was *still* the poor girl with the scruffy hair who was at the posh grammar school on sufferance—not because she was actually bright and deserved to be there.

When, one glorious Sunday morning during a walk in Hyde Park, Hayden had surprised Kate with an engagement ring she had honestly been stunned. He loved her, he had said, and had hardly been able to think about anything else other than getting her to marry him. She'd promised him she'd think about it—saying that it was perhaps too soon to agree to such a commitment when they had only known each other a few short months at the most. But Hayden had worn her down with his persistence and, finally convincing herself that he must indeed love her— even though her own feelings had still been less than clear—Kate had foolishly agreed to the engagement. In her own defence she'd still been in the early stages of bereavement, and she saw now that she had probably unconsciously been craving the love and attention she'd so long been denied. Maybe that was why Hayden's proposal and declaration of love had been so appealing?

The night they'd got engaged Kate had surrendered her virginity to her husband-to-be, and had even started to feel excited at the prospect of getting married and setting up a home together. But just one week later all her dreams of a happy future—of a devoted husband and longed-for children—had come crashing down around her ears with an ear-splitting crack.

The day it had happened Hayden had told Kate that he was flying out to Amsterdam on business, and that when he returned in the evening he would pick her up and take her to dinner at one of his favourite West End restaurants. But during the morning at work Kate had developed painful period cramps that had become progressively worse as time went on. By lunchtime she had felt quite ill with the pain, and her boss had told her to take the afternoon off and go home and rest. Hayden had had a house in an exclusive mews in Chelsea, and it was much closer to work than Kate's flat in north London. He had given her his spare key to hold on to, in case he ever got locked out, or if she got off work earlier than he did and needed to meet him there. As soon as she let herself into the low-ceilinged, stylish hallway, Kate's senses had immediately alerted her to the fact that the house was occupied.

Her heart pounding, in case the occupant turned out to be a burglar—Hayden hadn't rung her to say his meeting was cancelled—Kate had just been nervously and perhaps rashly negotiating the stairs that led to the bedrooms when she'd heard the unmistakable sound of female laughter. Holding tightly on to the stair-rail, her mouth as dry as wood-shavings, she had made herself go up to the main bedroom door and open it wide. There she had found her fiancé and a voluptuous redhead at least ten years older than herself in bed together.

Kate remembered standing there dazedly telling herself that what she saw could only be some bizarre figment of her imagination because she wasn't feeling well. As hard, cold reality had kicked in, like ice water being poured down her neck, she remembered she'd started to tremble from head to foot—partly in shock and partly in fury. But a worse shock was to follow, when Hayden had given her a disparaging glance, wiped his hand across his mouth and then laughed. *It was the coldest, most haunting laughter Kate had ever heard.*

'You stupid little bitch!' he'd declared. 'What the hell made you turn up here in the middle of the day?'

That was when Kate had discovered the man she had planned to marry was *not* the happy-go-lucky work-driven individual with a secret sensitive side that she'd believed him to be. That was when she had discovered Hayden Michaels was a liar and a cheat, with a lover he'd had for over two years who he had no intention of giving up. In fact he'd been furious that Kate had gone and ruined it all by turning up when she had.

Her throat locking in anguish, and too upset to say anything, Kate had flung his key onto the bed and left the house as fast as her legs would carry her…

The whole thing had been an embarrassing mess. She'd made an absolute fool of herself, falling for Hayden's lies, and for a long time afterwards she'd felt nothing but numb. When the opportunity had come a few months later to fly out to Italy and take a break with a colleague she had once worked with who had moved out there Kate had grabbed the chance with both hands.

That night at the party she hadn't wanted to go to—when she'd set eyes on Luca for the first time—she had been utterly stunned by the depth of longing she had experienced for a complete stranger. Overwhelmed by him—and by the longing he'd seemed equally to experience for her—and still smarting from her bitter experience with her ex, Kate had allowed herself to succumb to the Italian's expert and wonderful seduction. *But in the morning she'd got cold feet and, telling herself she'd probably just made another colossal mistake with a man, she'd fled before even giving herself time to talk to Luca or think things through…*

'I was—I was getting over a break-up with someone before I came out to Italy,' she said to Luca now.

The highly efficient air-conditioning in the room added to the chills already rippling through her body at having to recall the painful memories of that time.

'So you slept with me on the rebound? Is that what you are saying?' The bitter thread in Luca's huskily rich voice was easy to detect.

'No! That's not what I'm saying at all! I didn't sleep with you on the rebound!'

'Then I was some kind of consolation prize, perhaps? Because your boyfriend had rejected you?'

'Please just listen to me, will you?' Unfolding her arms, Kate moved nearer to the huge desk separating her from the glowering handsome man behind it. 'He didn't reject me…at least not in the way that you think. We'd just got engaged to be married when I found him in bed with another woman…his lover, as it turned out.'

Some of the tension in Luca's face seemed to depart, yet his arresting blue eyes were still full of suspicion, Kate noticed.

'Was he a wealthy man, this ex-fiancé of yours?' he asked.

'He was a successful broker in the City.'

'Many wealthy men have lovers. It is perhaps not as shocking as you think, Katherine.'

What was he telling her? That he too had a lover? Suddenly she could barely withstand the wave of misery that the possibility produced. Desperately trying to field her hurt and thinking that perhaps she really should get some therapy to help her stop making such poor choices in men, she let a heavy sigh escape her. *Could events get any worse?*

'Well, I think it's pretty shocking!' she declared with heat. 'If you can't trust the person you're intending to spend the rest of your life with, then who *can* you trust? He lied to me. Made me think he was a very different kind of man from the one he *really* turned out to be! I could not knowingly or willingly be in a relationship with a man who needed another woman on the side! The idea is abhorrent to me— and would be to most normal women, I'm sure!'

'That is your prerogative. But why did you leave my bed the next morning without telling me you planned to leave? That I still do not comprehend.'

'I was scared.' Kate shrugged, and inside her chest her heartbeat picked up speed a little too rapidly, making her dizzy. She was nauseous too, and a sudden urgent need to locate the nearest bathroom became absolutely imperative.

'Of what?' Luca questioned.

'Can't you guess? Of making a fool of myself with a man all over again! I'm sorry—but I really need to get to the bathroom!'

Turning hurriedly away from Luca's desk, Kate barely knew which direction her feet were taking her, and the sense of disorientation that washed over her made it hard for her to focus.

'Katherine?'

The sharp concern in Luca's voice surprised her, but Kate was too intent on getting to the bathroom before she disgraced herself more emphatically than she could bear to imagine to acknowledge it. Pushing open the sleek walnut twin doors of his office, she found herself in a thickly carpeted corridor. Without hesitation she headed straight for the women's cloakroom right at the end.

* * *

Alarmed at how suddenly Katherine's face had turned so ghostly white, Luca sprang up from the leather chair behind his desk and followed her to the ladies' washroom. Pushing open the door to the scented interior, he heard with alarm the sound of retching coming from one of the cubicles.

'Katherine!' he called out, following the direction of the sound. 'Are you ill? What is the matter? Tell me!'

'Please,' returned a wretched sounding voice, 'just leave me alone. I'll be all right in a minute.'

'Do you need help? We have a resident medic in the building. I will go and fetch her.'

'No! Please don't do that! I told you. I'll be okay in a minute. Just let me sort myself out, will you?'

Uncertain whether that was wise, nonetheless Luca realised he had no choice but to give her a few moments to recover from whatever had disturbed her and trust that it wasn't something serious.

Returning reluctantly to his office, he paced the floor a little, his body thrumming with impatient restlessness at not knowing what was wrong with her. In the time that he waited for Katherine to return from the bathroom he reflected on what she'd told him about her ex-fiancé and the fact that she had discovered him in bed with his lover.

'Innocent loveliness'—that was how his friend Hassan had described her at the hotel, and Luca silently agreed that that was certainly the impression her sweet face and quiet voice so beguilingly depicted. Yet Luca knew her to be a woman capable of the kind of passion that made a man's heart beat so fast he barely knew his own name when he was in her arms! A heady, irresistible torrent of heat suffused him at the memory. *Had she been telling him the truth when she'd told him the story of her ex and his mistress?* If she had, and she had really loved this man, then he could see how she would have been badly hurt by such a betrayal. But Luca did not know Katherine well enough to judge if she was speaking the truth or not.

All he knew was that her unexpected and sudden departure before he woke had confused and disturbed him, as well as making him question his own judgement. If she had tried to contact him to explain or apologise shortly afterwards he might—just might—have forgiven her. But in three months there had been nothing but silence where she was concerned, and now Luca was just as much in the dark about her as ever.

Katherine was the first woman in over three years, since Sophia had died, who had captured his attention, and her behaviour following their night together had been more than regrettable. There had been a sense of the most astonishing connection between them. And not just on a physical level, he recalled. Something about her had revived feelings in him that he'd thought were lying permanently dormant—either that or he had simply lost the ability to experience them because of what had happened. He had been numb to sensation for so long and then he had seen Katherine across that crowded room. The mere sight of her had astoundingly made the blood pump almost violently in his veins! How did one explain those mysterious things? Perhaps the truth was that she had caught him at a weak and emotionally vulnerable moment, and he had fantasised that the connection between them was far more meaningful than it really was?

Underlying his unhappy speculation was a longing to dig a little deeper into his own wounded psyche and discover the truth, yet the prospect honestly terrified him. Sighing, Luca rubbed an agitated hand round his clenched jaw. But then again, he concluded, his thoughts driving him near crazy, he was not unfamiliar with the rush of affection that could suffuse a man after he had made satisfying love to a woman. *Perhaps at the end of the day that was all it had been with Katherine?*

The doors opened behind him and Katherine stepped back into the room. Her face, though still too pale, did not look as alarming as it had when she'd run out. A genuine sense of relief swept through Luca.

'I'm sorry,' she apologised, rubbing her hand up and down one slender arm as though cold. 'I suddenly didn't feel very well. I'm better now, but I really think I need to eat something. I'll just pop across the road to the deli and get myself a sandwich.'

'There is no need for that! What you should do now is just sit down and rest for a while. I will arrange for some food to be brought up to my office.'

'It's all right. You don't have to do that.'

The telephone receiver already in his hand, Luca threw Katherine the steely look that he often utilised at business meetings when someone was being particularly obstructive. 'Yes, I do! It is fairly obvious that you need sustenance and rest, so you will do as I say, Miss Richardson, and not argue! *Capisce?*'

The selection of refreshments and drinks the catering manager personally brought up to Luca's office was more fitting for a visiting VIP than a temporary PA Katherine reflected in surprise when they were alone again. The food had been laid out on the highly polished table that was used for meetings, and tentatively they sat down opposite each other to eat it. After taking several small, hungry bites of a particularly delicious smoked ham and Dijon mustard sandwich on rye bread, Katherine felt the queasiness in her delicate stomach thankfully abate. But then she noticed that Luca was not eating at all. He seemed to be far more occupied with watching her instead.

Dabbing her linen napkin delicately at the corner of her mouth, she frowned. 'What's the matter? Aren't you hungry?'

'I will eat in a moment.' He shrugged.

His tie was still pulled away from his unbuttoned shirt collar, giving her an unwitting glimpse of a few fine, curling, dark hairs beneath the strong column of his tanned throat. Raised flesh stood out on Kate's bare arms in immediate response to that almost too tantalising detail.

'I am glad to see that your earlier distress has not adversely affected your appetite,' he commented.

'Luckily I'm one of those people who usually has a cast-iron stomach!' she joked. 'Not much adversely affects my appetite, I'm afraid!'

'Do not apologise for enjoying your food,' Luca replied with a genuine smile. 'It makes a pleasant change to meet a woman who does not regard food as the enemy!'

Kate's smile was more tentative than Luca's, and she had good reason. Quite aware that she had narrowly managed to avert disaster and keep him in the dark about her true condition in spite of her unexpected urgent dash to the washroom, she undeniably felt temporary relief at not having to explain things more fully. And she felt guilty about that. A big part of her was clamouring to just come out with it there and then, confess the *real* cause of her distress. However, somehow she didn't feel either ready or brave enough. *Besides,* Kate asked herself, *was it wrong of her to simply want to bask in the warmth and light of his gorgeous smile for just a little while longer rather than invite his disdain?*

CHAPTER FOUR

AT FIVE forty-five, Kate knocked on Luca's office door—the still ominously open office door—and braced herself to ask him if she had passed his one-day trial.

As far as the work went, she honestly thought things had gone without a hitch—but there was simply no guessing what Luca's decision would be. No doubt he was still getting over the shock of seeing her again, having her turn up to work for him—as Kate was him. After his thoughtful act of providing her with some much needed sustenance after her emergency dash to the bathroom he had more or less withdrawn into his office, only speaking to her when he had to. And that had consisted of little more than a couple of distracted *grazies* when she took him a cup of coffee.

'Come in!' he called out.

Taken aback to find him putting his arms into the sleeves of the elegant suit jacket he had hung on the back of his chair, clearly making ready to leave, Kate felt her heartbeat race a little in alarm.

'Are you leaving now?' she asked.

'Do you not think I have worked long enough today?' he retorted, with the wryest of reluctant smiles.

Warm colour poured into Kate's cheeks. 'I didn't mean that you shouldn't be leaving,' she said awkwardly. 'I only wanted to ask if I had passed your trial.'

'My what?' Luca's expression reflected definite puzzlement.

'You said you were giving me a one day-trial…presumably to see if I came up to scratch for the job?'

'Oh, *that*.' He shrugged dismissively, as if he had forgotten all about it. Then he levelled his gaze at Kate more seriously. 'Of course you must stay! It is not ideal, of course, but it is too late now for someone else to come in and learn the ropes. Besides…I need you to act as my hostess tonight, at the party I am throwing at my house.'

His calm assertion—as though he had already assumed that Kate would agree—slightly miffed her. As awkward as it might prove, she wanted to keep this job—of course she did. But she had been secretly looking forward to a long hot bath to help her wind down after the shocks and surprises of the day. Not to mention time to work out just when and how she was going to find the courage to tell Luca the astonishing secret she'd been nursing…

'You didn't say anything about that before!'

'I have had a lot of things on my mind today, Katherine. Not least of all *you*!'

He'd been thinking about her? Adjusting the strap of her leather bag on her shoulder, Kate wondered just what shape his reflections had taken. If they were anything like the conflicting thoughts and longings *she* had endured about *him*, then no wonder he had been preoccupied!

'Will you do it?' Luca asked now, with a frown creasing his faintly lined, tanned forehead.

And if she refused, risk losing both this job and the chance to tell him her news? Kate didn't reflect for long on her answer. 'Yes, I'll do it. But don't you have anyone else who could help out?'

'Janine would normally have stepped in, but as you know she is away on holiday and I am paying *you* to act as my personal assistant in her place—am I not?'

Detecting irritation in his voice, Kate did not want to antagonise Luca any further. But, although she was silently grateful that his need to have his personal assistant act as hostess suggested there wasn't currently a woman in his life, she was also curious as to why he remained single. The thought raised a ridiculously foolish hope inside her—*one that she quickly and painfully suppressed*.

'I'll have to go home first, to freshen up and change. What time will you need me there?'

'My chauffeur Brian will drive you home, wait for you, and then bring you back to the house. I will ride with you part-way and he can drop me off first. Come…let us go. Time is getting on.'

Regarding her expectantly, Luca put his hand behind Kate's back as he reached her, and disconcertingly—as if to remind her she really *was* playing with fire—a small electrical current fizzed through her at his touch.

Throwing the party at his house for Hassan, his associates, and a few business colleagues of his own along with their wives was not the strain that Luca had first envisaged. With a relentless work schedule that often included taking plans home to study and perfect he had been needing a holiday for quite some time now, but was deliberately resisting the fact. Now, as his interested blue eyes followed Katherine as she moved round his elegant drawing room, talking to his guests, he saw how easy his new personal assistant was making it for him this evening.

In a black cocktail dress, with her dark hair tumbling over her pale shoulders, adorned with only a simple diamante clip, she looked utterly ravishing. *Good enough to eat, in fact!* And Hassan's business associates had gravitated to her side time and time again after Luca had made the introductions, seeming reluctant to let her converse with anyone else, he noticed.

He knew his firm of architects were the elite of the elite, and that the businessmen would find it difficult to find another firm that could match the sheer innovation and high level of dedication to the client that his could, but he saw too that having Katherine as his hostess for the evening had gone a long way towards helping them make up their minds about giving him a commission. Having just had a conversation with them, sealing the deal with a handshake, and now alone again with his friend Hassan, Luca saw that he too was watching the lovely brunette across the room.

The older man smiled indulgently as she threw back her head and laughed at something amusing the wife of one of Luca's colleagues was saying to her. 'Do you know what an asset that beautiful woman is?' he remarked, not without a touch of envy in his voice.

People had used to say the same thing about Sophia, and Luca had felt a not insignificant burst of masculine pride that he was married to such a beauty. The thought made his stomach cartwheel. But they had not been so complimentary towards the end, he remembered soberly... Not when she had deliberately distanced herself from both Luca and company in general...

'I confess I did not realise how much until now,' he answered truthfully, contemplating the champagne in his glass with a distracted air. 'Certainly making everybody feel at home seems to come very naturally to her.'

'If I were you...' lowering his voice conspiratorially, Hassan drew nearer to the younger man '...I would definitely not let this one go!'

Later that evening, when his guests had departed and Luca found himself alone with Katherine, he could not help remembering what his friend had said, and he felt a definite reluctance in him to bid her goodnight. *No matter that she had not exactly been as keen to stay with him after their last meeting in Milan!* He'd be a liar if he did not acknowledge to himself that that still had the power to sting. But now, as she stifled a yawn and smiled at him apologetically, Luca felt strangely predisposed to forgive her....

'You did a magnificent job this evening,' he heard himself say, his stomach muscles tightening as he picked up the bewitching scent of her heavenly perfume. His glance skimmed the alluring decolletage of her dress, and he did not try to stem the heated desire that swept powerfully through him at the sight of that too tempting flesh. 'You were the perfect hostess!'

'Thank you.' Her dark eyes shied away from looking back at his too closely, he noticed. 'But it wasn't that difficult—not when you had invited such charming guests! Usually I don't find these kind of occasions easy at all!'

'Like at the party in Milan?' Luca suggested softly, reaching forward to wind a loose curl of her sable hair round his finger.

Katherine let out a surprised breath, and it skimmed over his skin like the gentlest of summer breezes.

'I confess I felt a bit like a fish out of water that night,' she admitted, a warm blush brightening her cheeks.

'You looked like a lost little girl who needed rescuing,' Luca concurred. 'But I felt equally lost that night.'

'At your own party?'

'*Sì*. Then I saw you…and strangely I felt lost no longer.'

Registering the shock in her lovely eyes, Luca suddenly woke up to what he was saying, and the sense of vulnerability his confession had provoked inside him. *Dio!* The champagne was dangerously loosening his tongue! Better let her leave now, before he made matters worse. He might find temporary solace in Katherine's arms again, but tomorrow he had to continue working with her— and sleeping with her, as much as he yearned to do just that, would only complicate things. Much better that he planned a sorely needed holiday than contemplate an affair with a woman who had already demonstrated to him she wasn't exactly trustworthy!

Releasing the delicate springy curl wound round his finger, Luca made a point of glancing down at his Rolex. 'It is getting very late, and we both have an early start in the morning. Brian is waiting in the car to drive you home.'

Choosing not to address the confusion mirrored in her gaze, Luca walked Katherine out into the chequered-floored hallway. Handing her her midnight-blue velvet cape, he helped settle it round her shoulders, employing every bit of willpower he could summon not to settle his hands there instead, and turn her round to face him so that he might kiss her as thoroughly as he longed to…

'Thank you again for your help this evening. I will see you at the office in the morning. Sleep well.'

'Goodnight, then,' she replied, her glance only briefly touching his, as though she had picked up his unspoken signal that it was better that they part and silently concurred with it.

Even as he opened the front door for her, Luca was mentally retreating. Watching Katherine walk down the concrete steps towards the silent gleaming Rolls Royce for only a moment, he closed the door behind her, as if to prevent himself from following her and fervently admitting that he would really like her to stay the night after all….

'Oh, God! Not again!'

Kate was typing a letter at her desk the next morning when a sensation of nausea overtook her, bringing her out in a clammy, cold sweat. Frantically reaching for her bag, she dug inside it for the dry biscuits she'd remembered to bring with her that day. Just as she located them, Luca walked into the room.

'I'd like you to ring this number in Paris for me.

It is the office of a client of mine and I need to—'
He cut off what he was saying to frown down with
concern at Kate's ghostly pallor.

In her anxiety she'd accidentally swept the biscuits in their flimsy cling-film wrapping onto the
floor, and as she reached out to retrieve them the heel
of her shoe connected instead. Kate knew they were
crushed even before she examined the evidence. At
that moment her nausea was suddenly made worse
by an overwhelming sense of despair. Rising up from
her desk, she bolted from the room without pausing
to explain to Luca where she was going.

'Katherine!' she heard him call after her, and she
registered the sense of frustration and bewilder-
ment in his voice even as she hurried away. 'Are
you ill again? What is the matter? *Dio!* Why will
you not tell me?'

By the time Kate felt well enough to return to her
office, it was to discover Luca staring out of the
window. The tension in his broad shoulders was
palpable as he stood with his back to her. Hearing
her come in, he turned to face her. His expression
was so haunted that Kate sucked in a shocked
breath. He looked like a man who had been shaken
from a dream—and a singularly unhappy one at
that. Something inside Kate rose up in protest at the

sudden idea that he was hurting, and she momentarily forgot the reason for her hasty dash to the bathroom. Almost.

'Luca? Are you all right?' she asked.

'It is me that needs to ask *you* that question!' he retorted, impatience edging his tone. 'Clearly something is *not* all right when you turn the colour of pure white marble and rush from the room! What is wrong with you, Katherine? And I do not want you to spare me anything! Just tell me the truth, will you?'

Taking a deep breath, and drawing out the chair behind her desk to sit down, Kate sighed and admitted softly, 'I'm pregnant.'

'You are *pregnant*?'

It wasn't a question that Luca responded with, merely an unaffected statement of fact that sounded rather distant and detached. The sensation of sluggish melting ice meandered slowly down Kate's back. Somehow his detachment sounded far more forbidding than outright anger—which, in truth, was what she had been expecting.

'By your ex-fiancé? Is that what you are telling me?'

His assumption took her aback for a moment.

'I broke up with him three months before we met, Luca…I'm only just twelve weeks pregnant.

So, no…he's *not* the father of my baby. That's not
what I'm telling you at all.'

'Then what you are trying to say is…that *I* am
the father?'

'Yes.'

Her fathomless dark eyes seared into his very
soul. Luca inhaled, and although he sensed and
heard his own sharp intake of breath, he felt more
like an observer, looking down at himself, rather
than the actual owner of the stunned unmoving
form that occupied his chair. A surreal moment
ticked by when his thought processes seemed frighteningly suspended from all sense of reality. Then
as he began to devastatingly react, long-frozen
feelings desperately tried to creep round the ice that
packed them.

The woman who sat in front of him, dark eyes
holding his with surprising steadiness in light of
the emotion she had just caused to erupt inside
him, waited for him to speak. How could she know
that Luca was seriously struggling right then with
the means to do that? When he did reply, his voice
sounded as though he had narrowly missed
choking on dust.

'And you expect me to believe this outrageous
claim?'

'You wanted the truth. Don't spare you anything, you said.'

As the fear icily gripped him that Katherine might be deceiving him—or, *worse*, trying to blackmail him into taking responsibility for another man's child—rage acted as extremely effective lubrication for Luca's dry throat.

'We only slept together once, *cara mia*—remember? It is over three months since I saw you last! How do I know how many men you have had in your bed since then?'

Instantly she looked as distraught as if Luca had struck her. But his sympathy was in short supply right then. He really *did* want the truth. Even if it was painful. *Was this woman he barely knew, yet who had caught him in her spell, even capable of giving it to him?* She had no idea of what turmoil and—perversely—what bittersweet hope her news had produced inside him because of his own painful journey to this juncture in his life. Even as she had jumped up and run from the room Luca's thoughts had inevitably gravitated to Sophia…to the tragic way she had lost her life… He had thought he couldn't bear it if he learned that Katherine might be taken from him, too.

'Whatever you believe, I'm not someone who

sleeps around!' she exclaimed now. 'What happened between us was like a bolt out of the blue…a once-in-a-lifetime event! I may still have been upset about what had happened with my ex, but I swear to you I didn't sleep with you on the rebound!'

'And you truly believe the child you are carrying to be mine?'

'I'm absolutely certain. It's not something I would make up. I—I'm not angling for money or anything like that! I just thought I owed it to you to tell you what had happened after I left. I swear I have no ulterior motives!'

'And yet you made little effort to contact me to tell me that you were pregnant? And even now it is not by design that you turn up in my office but, if I am to believe it, mere coincidence! What would have happened if you had not been given the assignment as my temporary PA? Answer me that! Exactly when were you planning to let me know of your condition, Katherine? When the child was born? When it was five, maybe ten years old?'

Luca walked abruptly away, then came slowly back again. He could not understand it! For Katherine not to have tried to contact him when she had first learned she was pregnant was enough to make him lose what little hold on patience and understanding he had left. Whatever her reasons for the unacceptable delay in getting in touch with him, this time Luca was going to make absolutely sure that she did not run away. Because, in spite of the fury and frustration he felt towards her right now, miraculously she had given him the one piece of news that he had for so long yearned to hear and had feared he never would... *At last he was to become a father.*

Still seated, and looking rather too pale again, Katherine touched her hand to her chest, as if to calm her racing heart. 'I would have told you as soon as I had found out if I could have! But the friend I went to your party with moved to the States and I had no way of contacting her. I couldn't remember the address of your mansion in Milan, and not knowing that you worked in London I didn't even think of trying to look for you here! I swear I racked my brains to try and think how to reach you, Luca...I mean it! But it just wasn't possible. Can't you imagine what turmoil I was in when I found out I was pregnant? It was a genuine shock! I was still on the pill...but there were a couple of days in Milan when I was so upset about things that I must have forgotten to take it. When I realised what had happened, and the result of it, I was honestly stunned! But I'm determined to keep the baby...

even if I have to raise him on my own! I wasn't expecting you to support me even if I *did* manage to contact you. I was wary of seeing you again when we had only known each other for just a night. And there…there was always the possibility that you might not even remember me!'

Sucking in his breath, Luca inadvertently bit the inside of his cheek. Ignoring the sting of pain, he silently dismissed the ludicrous suggestion that he might have forgotten her. After such a night together? Impossible! Last night, watching Katherine win over everyone in the room with her beauty and grace, Luca had known—despite what he had told her when she'd first arrived in his office—that he most definitely *did* want a repeat performance of that magical night they'd shared in Milan! But for some reason, feeling the need to guard his heart after his confession about feeling lost that night, he had not been ready to allow things to proceed in that direction. Now he made himself focus on the other possibility Katherine had just mentioned. *Raising the child on her own….*

The thought absolutely affronted his profound sense of honour and duty, to do what was right—not to mention the fact that this child would be the sole heir to his family fortune, all that Luca possessed! There was no way—no way on God's earth—that Katherine was going to raise this baby alone! If she thought that he was going to meekly stand aside after all the pain, devastation and bitter disappointment he had been through before he met her, and again after she had left, then he had to quickly and catagorically disabuse her of that idea!

'I will, of course, insist on a paternity test once the child is born, but for now I will accept what you say as the truth. I pray for your sake it *is* the truth, Katherine! That said, there is something that I need to make perfectly clear to you.'

Stalking across the room to the huge window that shared the same panoramic views as his own office, Luca did not have to dwell for long on what he wanted to say.

'There is no way that you are going to raise my child single-handedly, without my help. It is an unthinkable idea! Preposterous, in fact!' As he turned to face her again, his jaw resolute, Luca witnessed the indignant surge of heat that poured into Katherine's cheeks.

'There is something that *you* ought to know too,' she declared with a frown. 'I'm not unhappy that you want to take your share of responsibility in raising this baby—in fact, I am relieved to hear it!

But I'm not going to let you get all heavy-handed with me about it either! I've looked after myself for a long time now, and if you try to ride roughshod over my wishes I'll simply walk away and you'll never hear from me or the child again!'

So infuriated was Luca by Katherine's threat that before he'd realised even what was in his mind, he strode across the room to where she sat and roughly hauled her to her feet.

Her pupils dilated in shock. They were both breathing hard, but it was he who recovered first. How dare she have the audacity to threaten him with walking away when it was *his* baby that she carried? The idea that the one thing he had longed for above all else—a child—might be taken away from him before the infant was even born was like being threatened with a painful, slow death after all that he had endured. Blue eyes blazing, Luca brought his face just inches away from Katherine's—and for once the sight of her beautiful features and the seductive scent of her body did not have its usual powerful, bewitching effect on his libido.

'How dare you? How dare you throw such a threat in my face? I will forgive you for it just this once, because you clearly know no better, but make it a second time and I will drag you through every court in the land if I have to! And once the child is born *I* will be the one who has sole custody of his welfare. Mark my words, *cara mia*! I do not say them idly! Persist in this disagreeable vein and you will soon come to bitterly regret your foolishness in issuing me with such a warning!'

Her tender flesh throbbing with discomfort from where Luca's hard fingers had seized her arm, Kate felt her legs all but turn to jelly at the fury in his voice. This wasn't how she'd imagined him receiving the news of her pregnancy—becoming instantly possessive and threatening to haul her through the courts for sole custody should she dare to even suggest she might walk away and raise the child by herself! She had only said that because he had sounded so domineering, and a fear had suddenly consumed her that he might not turn out to be the man she'd yearned for him to be after all.

Guessing that her colossal mistake with Hayden had had a lot to do with her fear, she wondered if she could ever truly accept the possibility of a healthy relationship with a man? Something told her that Luca was decent—kind, even—but a man did not become as successful and powerful as he was without having a streak of ruthlessness. Right now she needed to concentrate on the serious prospect of having his baby—a baby Kate already loved with a passion that she could hardly believe. For that reason, if nothing else, they simply *had* to reach some kind of mutual understanding and respect for each other's wishes when it came to how he was going to be raised.

'Please let go of my arm.' Her gaze met Luca's with quiet, dignified resolve, but she was a hair's breadth away from tears. 'You're hurting me.'

Glancing down at her limb, as if only just becoming aware he was gripping it so tightly, he released it with a dark, unreadable look in his eyes. Letting fly a passionate Italian curse, he stalked away. Kate wasn't sure if it was she he was mad at or himself.

'I didn't know that you'd react like this,' she told him honestly, her voice not quite steady. 'There are plenty of men who'd run a mile if they found out they'd made some girl they'd only spent one night with pregnant! For all I know this could have been the worst news for you to hear if you were in a relationship with someone!'

'Well—' he grimaced, one corner of his mouth twisting ironically, '—luckily for you, Katherine, I am *not* in a relationship with anyone at the moment. And even if I were I would still claim responsibility for this child if it is mine, and I would definitely want to help raise it! Do not make the mistake of judging all men by the poor example of your ex-fiancé!'

Realising she had done exactly that, Kate said nothing.

'You crushed your biscuits,' he observed, frowning, staring at the forlorn packet on the floor. 'Let me ring Catering and ask them to bring you something to eat. I do not want you passing out from lack of nourishment! You are having a baby and you need to take care of yourself.'

A jolt of surprise zigzagged through Kate's insides at his words. That last sentence had sounded gruff, yet strangely tender too. She told herself she was probably just imagining it. Hormones making her overly emotional and all that…

'Please don't bother. I don't want anything to eat right now.'

'You are sure?'

'I'll eat something decent at lunch.'

'Well…in that case I think I will go out for a while,' he announced, his gaze restless. 'You will be all right?'

'What do you mean?'

'I mean…you will not be ill again?'

Kate flushed. 'No. I'll be fine, I'm sure. The sickness comes and goes, and thankfully it doesn't last all day.'

'Good. Then please take messages for me and tell whoever calls that I will get back to them as soon as I can.'

'Okay.'

Unconsciously rubbing her arm where Luca's steel-like grip had bitten into her, she glanced up to find him staring down at her with such a look of near-desolation in his troubled gaze that her foolish heart turned over in her chest and made her ache to go to him. There was so much about this man that she didn't know, and yet that night he had made love to her the connection between them had been almost beyond words. Was there no chance of making that connection again? Last night, when he had admitted that he had been feeling lost too at his party in Milan, Kate's heart had soared with sudden delirious hope. But then, when Luca had suggested that it was time for her to go home, that hope had been dashed.

'I will see you later.' Tearing his eyes away from her, he strode to the door and went out.

With the brisk March wind gusting round his ankles and cutting into his face, Luca pounded the London pavements that led to a nearby park with a steely-eyed grimace that would have put the fear of God into even the bravest soul, should one have been foolhardy enough to confront him. There was much to preoccupy his mind as he walked.

Katherine turning up in his office had been shock enough, but then to learn that she was pregnant! Was the baby really his? The fast pace he had set himself momentarily slowed as the twin swords of fear and doubt pierced his chest. He so wanted to believe her, yet he did not want to be made a fool of and accept her word for it without question...at least not until a paternity test could be done. And, despite her threat to walk away if Luca got too dictatorial about the baby's future, he had to find out for himself if there was a possibility that she was trying to blackmail him in some way. He was an extremely wealthy man, and there was certainly enough information in the public domain about him and the illustrious firm of architects he had founded for anyone daring or cunning enough to seize a chance to extricate money from him in some way.

What if Katherine had not broken up with this 'despicable' fiancé of hers after all? What if they had concocted some scheme together after she had slept with Luca, to persuade him to financially support a child that wasn't even really his? The mere idea made him sick to his stomach.

Pushing the thought angrily away, he spied an empty park bench under a spreading oak and walked across the grass to sit there. Dropping his head into his hands, he considered the other real possibility that what Katherine had told him was true and that the baby she was expecting *was* his.

How ironic and bittersweet that this should happen after just one night with another woman when he and Sophia had tried for three long years to have a child. His wife had endured many uncomfortable and sometimes painful investigations in order to try and discover why she could not conceive, and Luca himself had also voluntarily undergone tests. It had turned out that there was no reason he could not father a child with someone else, but for some reason Sophia's ovaries had not developed properly and there was no possibility of her ever becoming pregnant. *She had been devastated.* Luca's suggestion that they adopt had not eased her grief at the knowledge that she would never bear a child naturally, and a few weeks after the doctor's findings—when they had been holidaying with friends on their yacht—she had to all intents and purposes thrown herself overboard and drowned.

Had Luca's own strong desire for fatherhood added to Sophia's distress that she could not bear her husband a child? He had tried to reassure her that it did not matter, that they could still have a good life together, but she had not been convinced and their marriage had gone downhill fast after that. *There had just been no reaching her...*

Shaking his head to fend off the knife-like anguish that surged into his chest, Luca pushed impatiently to his feet and started to walk again. From now on, he decided grimly, he would be shadowing Katherine like a hawk. And if he got even the slightest hint that she was lying to him in any way she would not get off lightly for deceiving him....

CHAPTER FIVE

WOULD Luca come to believe that the baby really *was* his? Kate fretted. Priding herself on always being a very honest person, she hated the idea that he might think she was lying. Yet she could easily see why he might doubt her. The truth was she *had* left it too long to get in touch with him—and perhaps she really should have tried much harder to find him?

She would be lying if she said she hadn't had any fears surrounding telling him she was pregnant. A man as wealthy and influential as Gianluca De Rossi would hardly be interested in a relationship with a mere PA like Kate, she'd reasoned painfully. Having seen the incredible mansion he lived in, and witnessed for herself the opulent lifestyle he enjoyed, it was obvious they were poles apart in almost every way she could think of! It still seemed like a miracle to Kate that Luca had set his sights on her that night, when there had been so many more stunning women to choose from! Women dressed to kill in outfits that probably would have cost Kate more than a year's wages! And, no…not even *one* of them had had the courtesy to speak to Kate. They had probably guessed from the outset by her shop-bought dress that she was nobody important.

To give Luca his due, *he* hadn't treated her like that. Which made it even sadder that she had let herself be beset with doubt and fear that he would ultimately reject her when she woke up to find herself in his bed. That chilly but sunny December morning in Milan Kate should have been feeling on top of the world after the pleasure Luca had given her, but instead she'd let those old debilitating feelings of inferiority get too much of a grip. Feelings that had been exacerbated by her grief over her mother's death and what had happened with Hayden. And when she'd returned to her friend's apartment to pack for her flight home she'd desperately tried to convince herself that Luca wouldn't give her a second thought when he woke and found her gone….

When he returned she was busy typing letters. The door opened suddenly in the outer office, and Kate heard it slam. She tensed as she heard him stride

across the room to his desk, and her shoulders practically flew up around her ears when he made a
detour almost straight away into her room. With
him he brought the earthy scent of the outdoors,
and his dark hair was boyishly ruffled, she noticed—
if not by his fingers, then by the elements.

'Any messages?'

For a moment, the intensely blue eyes that bored
into hers made her fall into a trance. Would her
baby inherit that same divine colour? she mused.

'Just a couple… Clients returning calls, but
nothing urgent.' She tore off a page from the pad
she'd scribbled on and handed it to him.

His glance was brief, almost dismissive. 'Like
you said, nothing urgent.' Scrunching up the paper,
he threw it into the wastepaper basket. 'I have been
walking in the park,' he told her.

'Oh, yes?'

'I have been doing a lot of thinking.'

Her throat swelling with tension, Kate said nothing.

'And I have made some important decisions.'

Still Kate remained mute, but she had the definite
feeling that her life was about to take a new
dramatic turn and her heart skipped a beat.

'I have decided that you cannot continue working when you are clearly not well and need proper

rest. I have been needing to take a break from work myself for some time also. Therefore I propose that we go back to Italy for a while. The atmosphere there will be much more conducive to rest and relaxation, and the sooner we can leave the better. Tomorrow would be ideal.'

Staring at him in astonishment, Kate marvelled at his skill in making such a potentially contentious statement with such apparent ice-cool calm! As if he were merely saying to her, *Take a letter, Miss Richardson* instead of *Risk everything…your job, your livelihood, your way of life…and fall in with my plans wherever they might lead you!* But even though she sensed many obstacles ahead if she were to comply, Kate also sensed a jolt of excitement go through her at the idea of returning to Italy with Luca.

'It's not that I'm unwell,' she said reasonably. 'I'm pregnant—that's all!' Even as the words left her mouth, she thought about the genuine toll early pregnancy had taken on her body and mind, and realised she would welcome a holiday…however short or long. But the unresolved issues between her and Luca nevertheless made her less than easy about the prospect.

'Yes, you are pregnant,' he acknowledged, with a flash of what appeared to be concern in his vivid blue eyes. 'And I do not think it best for you or the baby for you to be putting yourself under the unnecessary duress of working full-time when you do not have to!'

'Do you think I'm working just for the fun of it, then?' Kate burst out, her ingrained sense of independence and self-sufficiency kicking in like a well-oiled machine that had never been given the chance to get rusty. 'How else do you think I can earn the money to support myself?'

'From now on *I* will be taking care of all that. If it is *my* child you carry in your womb, then it is only right and fair that as the father I support and look after you both! I will ring the agency, explain what is happening, then arrange for our flights to Milan tomorrow. I suggest we leave the office around five today and go back to my house in Mayfair. We will have something to eat together and then I will take you home so that you can pack for our trip.'

Having never had anyone say they would take care of things and look after her before, Kate silently acknowledged how appealing Luca's declaration was. *If more than a little scary!* Could she trust that he would keep his promise when they got to Milan? That he wouldn't regret it? Telling herself that he too was taking a massive leap of faith by trusting her enough to even suggest she return to Italy with him, Kate decided she would give his proposition a try.

'All right, then.' Folding her hands in her lap, she experienced at that moment an unusual sense of calm. It was as though by reaching a decision to fall in with his suggestion she was letting fate take control rather than try and fight it. *Mainly because she was weary of fighting and weary of being afraid.*

Luca quirked a dark eyebrow at her response, clearly surprised. 'You agree?'

'Yes, I agree.'

'Katherine? It is after five o'clock and time we left.' The demands of work had helped the afternoon pass surprisingly quickly, and thankfully had left Kate little time to brood over her decision to go to Italy. Now suddenly Luca was behind her, holding out her jacket so that she could slip her arms into it, and she was so flustered by his nearness that it took two tries before she was finally able to pull it on. As she turned to thank him, he completely astonished her by reaching out his hand and touching the tips of his fingers to her stomach.

'You hardly show at all yet,' he remarked, a disconcertingly husky catch in his voice.

Kate sucked in a breath, speech seeming to desert her. The faint brush of his fingers was enough to set her heart pounding and propel volcanic heat searing right through her core. Her need for him to touch her again became all-consuming, like a silent powerful mantra trembling in her blood. *Touch me…please touch me.*

'I expect I'll start to show a bit more any day now.' Lifting her shoulders in a self-conscious shrug, Kate prayed that she'd been quick enough to draw a veil down over her longing so that Luca hadn't seen it. What was it about this man that made her unravel? The compelling authority he wielded over her senses was like a powerful force of nature she'd never encountered before.

'You look a little tired,' he remarked, closely studying her features with concern, and registering the faint darkened circles beneath Katherine's eyes with disagreeable shock. Regret radiated through Luca that he had not noticed her fatigue earlier. If he had been in any doubt about his decision to take her back to Italy so that she could get the rest she needed, all his doubts were suddenly and forcefully allayed.

Pregnancy took its toll on a woman's body. Pregnant women tired more quickly and were prone to becoming emotional. Therefore, besides eating well and avoiding stress, rest was a key factor for the mother-to-be. That was one of the things Luca had learned from the many medical books he had avidly read in his and Sophia's desperate quest to have a baby of their own. Tragically, pregnancy was not a condition that his wife had been destined to experience, so there had been no opportunity for him to lavish the care and attention on her that he would have loved to if their hopes had become a reality.

'Come…let us see about getting you home.'

His hand now solicitously at the small of Katherine's back, Luca led her from the office to his personal elevator just down the hall.

The under-floor heating that radiated from the exquisite parquet flooring deliciously warmed Kate's stockinged feet as she carried her glass of fresh pomegranate juice across the room with her. In Luca's modern, interior-designed living room, the most breathtaking collection of art—stunningly lit—decorated the muted tone walls.

When she'd acted as his hostess the previous night she had barely had time to consider the paintings, because etiquette had demanded she give her full attention to Luca's guests. But now, narrowing her intrigued gaze at a portrait that took pride of place, she caught her breath as she realised this was no faithfully reproduced print or copy but the *real* thing. The artist was a Renaissance painter that Kate had studied for her final-year art exam at school, and she'd seen the painting before only in a book. That was why it had immediately commanded her interest. Its monetary worth must be in the region of *millions* of pounds!

A frisson of shock ran up her spine. Having visited Luca's mansion in Milan, she was well acquainted with the fact that the man must be in an elite bracket of extremely wealthy individuals. But to see a priceless painting in his living room was almost surreal!

'Ah…you are enjoying viewing my little gallery of Italian art, I see.'

So enraptured by the artwork, Kate hadn't even heard Luca enter the room, let alone practically reach her side before she registered he was there. On their arrival at the stunning Mayfair townhouse, he had dismissed his housekeeper for the evening, brought Kate the fruit juice she had asked for, and very soon after had gone down to the wine cellar to select a bottle to go with the meal that had been left for them to eat when they were ready. Now he had reappeared and, withdrawing her attention from the painting, Kate was momentarily silenced by the sight of him.

He had changed into casual chinos and a loose white shirt, and his tanned feet were bare. The breathtaking profile of sculpted, masculine beauty that was hers to savour and appreciate was in serious competition with the arresting woman in the portrait. So much so that Kate's womb contracted with an almost shocking sense of violent sensual awareness in response.

'How could I not?' Answering his question, Kate clutched the glass in her hand as if to anchor herself in some sort of reality. 'I studied this painting at school, so I know it well. Learning about the artist and how he worked was fascinating! If things had been different I would have loved to have studied art properly, perhaps even made a career of it.'

'What stopped you?'

'I simply couldn't afford to spend time in further education. I come from a single parent family and I needed to work to help bring in some money.'

'What a pity,' Luca remarked. 'But commendable too. I can tell by the tone of your voice that you are clearly passionate about the subject. It must have been quite a sacrifice to give it up!'

'Not really. I've learned that life doesn't always

work out the way we'd like it to…but that's okay. I don't consider myself deprived in any way. I was able to help my mum when she needed me, and that's all that matters. Hopefully, there'll be other opportunities as time goes on.'

'I do not doubt it.'

'This painting…aren't you afraid somebody will break in and steal it?'

'I am impressed, Katherine, that you have detected it is the real thing and not merely a copy.' As he smiled at her, Luca's arresting blue eyes glimmered like priceless sapphires. 'But do not be concerned about anyone breaking in to try and steal it. There is a state-of-the-art security system installed that is probably even more secure than the one protecting the Crown Jewels! I have the painting on display because great art should be on view, not hidden away in some vault! This way my friends can enjoy her beauty as well as myself.'

'I'm glad you feel that way. She's completely compelling!' Kate breathed, a genuine rush of true appreciation flowing through her veins as she turned back to the portrait of the sultry brunette.

'Hair the stunning black of a clear winter's night, eyes the colour of the world's most luxurious bitter chocolate…and lips—lips that were made for amore... An altogether sensual and stirring combination that is quite irresistible! She reminds me of someone I know.'

Luca's voice had turned warm as the amber gold of cognac heated over a flame, and all Kate's senses leapt into vivid life as though his words had physically caressed her. 'Really?' Quickly she took a sip of the sharp chilled pomegranate juice to ease her suddenly parched throat.

'You know I am talking about *you*, Katherine? You are easily as lovely as the beautiful *Margherita*.'

'Now you're mocking me!' Embarrassed heat washed over her that Luca would praise her looks so lavishly. Many years ago, when she'd first seen a print of it, Kate had been mesmerised by the portrait—and to suggest that she in any way resembled the lovely creature depicted was nothing but pure unbelievable fantasy, in her opinion! But the man beside her was regarding her as though genuinely perplexed.

'I did not make the comparison glibly, and I am certainly not mocking you! I meant every word,' he insisted.

Of course he did! Kate cynically reflected. Men would say anything to get a woman into bed. Some men were even prepared to fake being in love to get what they wanted! And even then *one* willing woman wasn't enough! Recalling with dismay that Luca had not been at all shocked by the revelation that Kate's ex-boyfriend had had another lover, she now found herself desperately needing to know if he had one. Was she being totally naïve in hoping that he did *not*? He had claimed that he was unattached, but—being intimately acquainted with his passionate nature—it did not strike Kate that he was a man who would happily go without a woman in his bed for long. How would she handle the news of a lover when her attraction for him had grown into a ceaseless yearning she could barely contain? And in the not too distant future she was going to give birth to his baby. Was she destined to be always on the periphery of some man's life and not at the centre, as she so desired?

'Katherine?'

'Let's talk about something else, shall we?' Affecting a careless shrug, Kate suddenly found she needed some breathing space. Moving across the room, she went to sit down on one of the sumptuous leather sofas by a ravishing Persian rug containing all the sensuous exotic colours of a Marrakesh bazaar in its hand-woven threads.

'Tell me what is troubling you.'

It shouldn't have surprised her that Luca would notice her unease, but somehow it did. In her limited experience of men, Kate had discovered most of them gave the discussion of personal issues a very wide berth. But apparently Luca was not one of those men.

Now he dropped down easily onto the sofa opposite hers, with a sensual loose-limbed elegance that transfixed her. It would have been so easy to just sit there, paying silent homage to the kind of heaven-sent looks a woman conjured up in her dreams, but Kate was suddenly in no mood to be so easily distracted. She might have agreed to go to Italy for a while with Luca, but a holiday together was no guarantee of a shared future, and suddenly she found herself feeling quite desolate about that. She had personal knowledge of how tough it could be as the child of a single parent, and her dreams of having children had always included the father being permanently in the picture.

Placing her half-finished glass of juice on the stylishly designed coffee table by her side, Kate tucked one slender leg beneath her and faced Luca with an unwavering stare. 'I need to know what will happen after I've had the baby. You indicated before that you wanted to help raise the child, and I need to know what arrangements we're going to come to if that's the case. I can't spend the next six months in limbo!'

'I agree. And if the baby is indeed mine then I am only too anxious to put some firm arrangements in place too.'

The equivalent of a large cold stone seemed to sink inside Kate's stomach. *He still didn't believe that the baby she was expecting was his.* Misery filled her. How could she bear to wait until a paternity test could be done to prove to him she was telling the truth? Underlying her frustration was a growing sense of anger at not being believed.

'I don't know what I can tell you to convince you that what I'm saying is true. You seem determined to prove me a liar!' In an unguarded moment Kate let the despair and strain of the past few months creep into her voice. Months when she had berated herself regularly for not leaving Luca a forwarding address or a number that morning in Milan.

When she saw Luca rise up from his seat and move towards her, she really did not know what to expect. Suddenly she found herself staring fixedly down at his undeniably sexy tanned bare feet, with tears swimming hotly into her eyes. Taking her hands in his, Luca silently coaxed her into standing.

'I do not want to distress you further, but trust has

to be built, *cara mia*, and a man like me has perhaps more to lose than you realize, hmm?'

'You were the one that insisted you wanted to support this baby when I told you I was pregnant! It's not as though I'm hanging around hoping for a relationship or anything! That's the very *last* thing I need after what happened to me!'

'But, putting aside the baby, and the fact that you do not want a relationship,' Luca breathed throatily, smoothing some soft dark strands of hair away from where they fell against her cheek and then doing the same with her tears, 'what about this irresistible force that keeps on drawing us together? What do you want to do about *that*, Katherine? Ignore it?'

CHAPTER SIX

How could she ignore her own passionate nature?
Kate had always sensed it was there, lurking
beneath the prison of clothes and conformity, but
since that night with Luca in Milan this ache beyond
all aches had nagged away at her, until she was
afraid she could not turn her back on its call one
more second. And it would no longer allow her any
peace when this man was near.

So when Luca asked her if she intended to ignore
this 'irresistible force' between them, there was no
question in Kate's mind that she had to give an
honest answer.

'No,' she whispered hoarsely, laying the flat of
her palm against his faintly roughened cheek. 'I'm
not going to ignore it…I think that would be…
almost impossible.'

Warm, hard fingers circled the fragile bones of her

wrist and authoritatively moved Kate's arm to her side. With an almost feral sound that seemed to rise up from his very soul Luca seared her lips with a reckless untamed kiss that shocked her. Completely lacking in finesse or tenderness, it made her reel with its almost ruthless demand. But that did not stop her from responding to it with equally raw hunger and need. The flame inside her that had been steadily simmering beneath her every day burst suddenly into an inferno…a scorching hot fire that would raze anything standing in its path to the ground.

Her arms went hungrily round Luca's neck to help deepen the erotic consummation of lips and tongues, fierce sighs and rasping moans, as liquid heat poured into her centre, making all her muscles tremble with the forceful devouring need that ravished her. Luca's feverish hands were tracing every inch of her through the mutually unwanted barrier of her clothing, and Kate sensed his impatience and ardour build at pace with her own, until its heated, unconstrained rhythm dictated they lose themselves totally in its potent wild current.

Somehow he removed her dress and she his shirt. Losing her balance in the fever of lust that consumed them, Kate felt the soft plumped-up surface of the sofa cradle her fall, and Luca's arms were firmly around her waist as they tumbled headlong together. His dark hair was tickling her face and his beard-roughened jaw was scratchy against her soft skin. The heavy, muscular press of his strong, hard body was so wonderful she could have cried. The ache that nothing could ease but him rejoiced in gratitude.

'I want you so much,' he vowed hoarsely against the side of her cheek. 'Too much!' And a husky litany of sensual sounding endearments voiced purely in Italian followed as his hands purposefully worked her tights and panties down over her quaking legs.

Consumed by sensation, by the wild earth scent of his body, Kate pushed her fingers through the short silky strands of his hair, then brought her hands lower to trace the sculpted indentations that denoted his cheekbones. Cupping his face, she accepted his kisses with unashamed eagerness, inciting more with her own teasing, searching tongue and softly rasping murmurs of pleasure.

Removing her bra, he kissed and suckled her breasts, and they were so tender that Kate sensed a sting of pain shoot through her when he nipped her gently with his teeth. As if realising her sensitivity, Luca stroked the tips of his fingers back and forth across the moist bud at her apex instead, and Kate's slender thighs opened and softened even as her whole body momentarily tensed in exquisite electrifying shock at his boldly intimate caress. Almost unbearably aroused, and driven by the raw, elemental nature that had irresistibly revealed itself that very first time with Luca, Kate splayed her hands against his chest, touching the sleek, warm musculature that was breathtakingly revealed beneath the silky dusting of soft dark hair.

But he didn't allow her to continue her exploration for long before guiding her hands purposefully down to the straining zipper on his chinos instead. In a heartbeat, his hard satin length was inside her, pressing upwards and deep into her melting warmth, and in the vivid heat and wild pleasure of their coupling Kate's heart lifted with hope—her whole being rejoicing to the heavens that she could be with him like this again.

Even before Luca's powerfully strong body had possessed hers, Kate's senses had been all but screaming for release. Pregnancy seemed to have doubled her sensitivity and awareness where he was concerned, until even just the scent of his cologne could practically unravel her. And now, as Luca drove into her, staking his powerful claim on Kate's body and soul for ever with his scalding unforgettable heat, her release came—quick and fast—making her shiver and shake as she was deluged by sensations and emotions that stole her breath and made her gasp and pant for air. Grabbing on to her lover's powerful shoulders, she kissed the smooth satin flesh that moulded that taut muscle and bone and shut her eyes tight, as if to guard and contain these almost *too* vulnerably intimate moments for ever.

He had been impatient with her all day. Impatient with the fact she was still wearing clothes, when Luca's intense desire was to separate her from them as soon as he could. To tear away every flimsy barrier that seemed like a fortified wall, preventing him from seeing her lovely perfection and touching her body as he so desperately yearned to.

Now he was where he wanted to be, the sensation was like lightning crashing, and the soft deluge of sweet summer rain breaking over his naked, hungry, overheated body in an unstoppable downpour. With the powerful physical release of orgasm had come the onrush of long-held in emotion and the breaking open of the desolation that Luca had experienced leading up to and after his wife's death. Suddenly it was exposed to the light, and shockingly he struggled with keeping away his tears.

He had not cried since he was a small child... not even at Sophia's funeral. Instead, he had withdrawn from the world for a while as much as he could, and isolation and loneliness had become familiar companions after she had gone. His parents had died too, so there was no one to console him. It had taken him quite some time to reconnect with people again. Work had been Luca's refuge and his solace. *Was it wrong of him to desire this woman so much—a woman who swore it was his baby she carried in her belly— when her touch right now was as essential to him as his breath?* Should he feel even guiltier than he was already that his wife had not been able to bear the child they had both longed for? Had he not suffered enough that he still had to pay for what had happened?

Katherine's mouth was at his shoulder, and the tender little kisses she was delightfully bestowing upon him commanded that it was *she* and not his past he concentrate on. A sense of grateful relief shuddered through Luca, dispersing his melancholy, and with it came a fragile yet tangible sense of peace.

Examining Katherine's face as she drew back to

glance up at him, her lips tenderly swollen from the passionate kisses they had shared and her dark eyes shimmering like starlight, he knew at that moment that her beauty easily surpassed the lovely *signorina* in the painting.

'*Come sei bella,*' he drawled, the corners of his mouth lifting in a seductive little smile. 'Look at you. How lovely you are!'

His gaze moved lower, to her smooth-skinned belly with its just discernible round curve, and he laid his hands over it, silently marvelling that the seed of a child—please God, *his* child—was flowering inside. A new, more alarming thought suddenly pierced him. What if he had been too passionate in his lovemaking with Katherine? What if he had unknowingly caused some potential harm to the growing infant?

'What's the matter?'

He had not been quick enough to hide his concern from his lover's watchful glance, and she lightly stroked his arm as if to minister comfort even before he answered. 'I didn't hurt you…or the child?'

'What?' Her slight frown was quickly followed by a smile that was like the dawn breaking. 'Of course you didn't! It's all right, Luca. It's perfectly safe to make love when a woman is pregnant—and I'm over the three-month mark now, so there's nothing to worry about.'

'You are sure?' Still guilt weighed heavy on him.

'Of course I'm sure.'

At last he let himself relax, and the sight of her sweet face, and her irresistible scent that seemed to permeate his skin, easily started to arouse him all over again.

Just before lowering his head to steal another hungry kiss, Luca glanced enquiringly into Katherine's soulful dark gaze. 'Are you hungry?' he asked her, smiling.

Her dark gaze shyly looked away.

'I mean for food!' he chuckled, delighted by her understandable misinterpretation. 'I said I would give you dinner, and Luisa, my housekeeper, has cooked authentic Italian pasta in your honour!'

'Can it wait a little while longer?'

'Sì…it can. I only have to heat it in the oven, so we can eat whenever we like. What did you want to do in the meantime, hmm?' he teased.

Focusing her eyes more boldly back on his, Katherine gave a softly anticipatory sigh, which feathered across Luca's already waiting mouth.

'Correct me if I'm wrong…but weren't you just

about to kiss me again?' she whispered, and his lips sealed hers even before she had finished speaking…

Later that evening, as Luca's chauffeur-driven Rolls-Royce pulled up outside the crumbling age-worn edifice of the Victorian end-of-terrace where Kate's ground floor flat was situated, she turned to the man sitting beside her with a suddenly self-conscious frown.

'What time did you say we were leaving tomorrow?'

'Our flight leaves around two-thirty, so I would probably say one…one-thirty at the latest. Why?'

'Look…it's going to take me a while to pack everything I need. Why don't I meet you in the morning instead of coming back with you tonight? Then you won't have to wait for me and I won't feel under pressure to rush.'

'The last thing I want you to do is rush! The whole point of us going to Milan is that you do not feel under pressure to do anything but rest, Katherine! If need be I can arrange for our flight to go later. It is my private jet, so it will not be a problem!'

'Your—your private jet?' she stammered.

'Of course!' he said, as matter-of-factly as though he'd just suggested getting a train.

Several thoughts went through Kate's mind at the same time. The predominant one being that she'd be an utter fool to think that their little sojurn in Italy would be more than a holiday. A man as incredibly wealthy and influential as Luca would not want to be saddled with an ordinary little nobody for long…she was sure of it. Even if she *was* having his baby. Back on his home turf, in his fabulous mansion, he would quickly see that Kate did not fit into such an elite lifestyle. That she was homespun…not priceless silk!

After their sensually charged evening together at his house she felt cold and deflated. Like a popped, discarded party balloon. Forcing a smile to her lips, she tried hard to conceal her inner turmoil. 'Well, I'll ring you in the morning, then…when I'm ready. Is that all right?'

'It is perfectly all right, *mi bella.*' Leaning towards her, Luca cupped her face in his hands, his warm breath skimming sensually over her mouth. 'You promise you will not let me down, Katherine?'

'What do you mean?' Even though she'd been the recipient of his wonderful touch all evening, Kate's senses thrilled to experience it again.

'If you do not come back with me tonight, you will not run away without telling me where you are?'

She shouldn't have been surprised that he was still dwelling on what had happened in Milan but, caught off guard, Kate was. *Surprised and more than a little pleased that he actually sounded as though he cared...*

'No, Luca. I won't be running away. I promise.'

'Good!' Warm lips grazed hers, sending shivers of unstoppable delight right through the heart of her, and he smiled ruefully when he eventually made himself pull away. 'Now, go inside and get some rest. You are looking tired again.'

'I'm only tired because it turned into a much longer night than I expected!'

Quick to reassure him that she was feeling fine, Kate still couldn't help colouring hotly as she thought about the highly sensual ways in which she and Luca had kept themselves occupied all evening. Her body ached and throbbed from her lover's seductive attentions still, and the memory of them would probably keep her awake for most of what was left of the night, she was sure!

'*Sì*...it did' His sexy blue eyes glanced back at Kate with disarming frankness, and in response the tips of her breasts surged almost painfully against the suddenly too thin material of her dress and jacket.

'I'd better go.' Turning towards the passenger door

at her side, Kate looked round in surprise as Luca caught hold of her wrist to hold her back for a moment.

'You will need to do your packing in the morning now. Are you sure you do not want me to stay over so I can help you?'

As enticing as the invitation was, right then Kate needed thinking space. So much had happened in the short time since she'd seen Luca again, and the repercussions were making her head spin! Plus, she didn't really want his distracting presence beside her when she came to selecting which clothes to pack for their trip. In his world—where women went to top designers to purchase their clothes—the reality of Kate's wardrobe would no doubt come as a bit of a shock—and no doubt a disappointment too.

Again it crossed her mind that when they returned to Milan the comparisons between her very ordinary way of life and his exceptionally wealthy and *extraordinary* one would inevitably start to become more pointed as the days went by. Once he was back in the realm of his equally fabulously rich friends, the stark differences would start to make themselves all too clear, and Luca would surely only come to regret bringing Kate with him?

'I'd rather do my packing myself, if you don't

mind?' she replied, shrugging. 'But thanks for offering.'

'Then sleep well, Katherine.' He moved back into the luxurious butter-soft leather seat with his usual enviable ease, his stunning good looks that next to other mere mortals could make them look shockingly plain in perfect harmony with the unashamed opulence of the car's interior. 'In the morning take as long as you need to get ready then ring me, yes? I will come and pick you up.'

'I will. Goodnight, Luca.'

He blew her a kiss and all but made her legs turn to water….

Awake long before the dawn, Luca had restlessly paced his bedroom and then the high-ceilinged rooms of the drawing room and kitchen as he tried to come to terms with the great frustration that gnawed away at him because Katherine had not slept in his bed.

One would think that once he had made love to her again his body would be satisfied, but *no*. All it had done was remind him of what he had been missing and indeed *craving* all these months without her! Now, instead of feeling refreshed and renewed from a good night's sleep, Luca felt bad-tempered and impatient—and his mood was not helped by the idea that Katherine might not keep her word about ringing him…that she might indeed decide at the last minute *not* to accompany him to Milan after all.

Why had he let her go back home so easily? Why had he not insisted he stay the night and waited for her to pack the next morning?

Thinking about the coming baby, and what any new desertion would mean to him, Luca swore softly but vehemently under his breath. He was not acting like a man who wasn't sure that his lover's baby was his at all. *On the contrary…* He was behaving as if there was no question that he was the father of Katherine's child!

Thinking of her passionate, uninhibited response to his lovemaking, Luca suddenly didn't doubt it. Something deeply intuitive, some strong inner sixth sense, finally convinced him that she was telling him the truth. Consequently he told himself it was only natural that he should feel so fiercely possessive about the child, and be beyond furious at the thought of her keeping it from him. But then there was this…this *addiction* he had developed for Katherine herself. He could neither easily explain it nor *want* to! In fact it was probably a good thing that they were at least compatible in that area, Luca concluded broodingly. It would certainly make things a lot more simple when he put to her the idea that had slowly been taking shape in his mind in the early hours when he could not sleep!

Several hours later, as he put down the phone at the end of a call to his office, his gaze morosely followed his chauffeur Brian as he carried Luca's luggage outside, to store in the back of the waiting Rolls-Royce. Glancing down again at the time on his watch, he vented his impatience out loud.

'*Dio!* What does she think she is playing at?'

What was making him even more on edge was the fact that he had rung Katherine's number three times already but there had been no reply. Not allowing his mind to descend into worryingly negative assumptions about the reason for her absence, or her delay in ringing him, Luca made up his mind to take action.

About to follow Brian out to the car and instruct him to drive to Katherine's flat, he heard the telephone on the hall table ring. Luca pounced on it, his heart hammering hard in his chest.

'De Rossi!' he snapped.

'Luca?'

'Katherine! Why have you not rung me? Where have you been? I have been ringing you all morning!'

'I'm in the hospital,' she returned, her voice definitely sounding a little shaky.

'The hospital? What is wrong? What has happened?' Feeling his blood turn to ice, Luca gripped the receiver hard, his knuckles turning white.

'I'll tell you when I get back home,' she replied, sounding a little more in charge than before. 'I've got a taxi waiting to take me, so I'll see you there.'

'Katherine!'

But the disconnect signal sounded in Luca's ear before he could get a response....

CHAPTER SEVEN

As soon as Kate saw the familiar Rolls-Royce parked outside the building where she lived, with its uniformed chauffeur in the front, all her limbs seemed to turn as insubstantial as cobwebs. As her footsteps slowed helplessly, her anxious gaze fell upon Luca's tall, arresting figure in a black cashmere coat, impatiently standing on the concrete steps that led up to Kate's front door.

As soon as he saw her approach the tension she sensed in him began to reach out and envelop her. Sucking in a deep breath for courage, and feeling a little light-headed, she made herself walk forward.

'Hi!' she called out, absently fingering the keys in her pocket and shivering as a blast of cold March air suddenly whipped her hair across her face. 'I'm sorry if I worried you when I wasn't here to answer your phone calls.'

His long legs making short work of the flight of steps, Luca planted himself in front of Kate with such a look of fear and apprehension in his eyes that for a moment it took her aback.

'Why were you at the hospital, Katherine?' he demanded, hands curving possessively round the tops of her arms in the thin navy raincoat she wore. 'I have been going out of my mind ever since you rang!'

'We'll talk inside shall we? It's not something I particularly want to discuss standing here outside in the rain.' Squinting up at the sky as icy droplets of moisture started to fall, Kate gave him a wobbly smile.

Reluctantly releasing her, Luca broodingly accompanied her back to the entrance of the house. Once inside the high-ceilinged Victorian hallway of her flat, Kate unwound the pink mohair scarf she wore from round her neck and looped it over one of the hooks on the coat-stand. Then she removed her now dampened raincoat to accompany it.

'Do you want to give me your coat?' she asked Luca as he stood there, his enviable Mediterranean tan appearing somehow less vibrant this morning.

'You should have called me!' he said accusingly, completely ignoring her outstretched hand. 'You were at the hospital, you said? What is the matter? Is it the baby?'

'Why don't we go and sit down?' Trying to stay as calm as possible, even though her stomach was churning, Kate led the way into the comfortable living room that she'd decorated with such loving care in the five years she'd lived there. Approaching the plain oatmeal couch, with its sunburst of brightly coloured cushions, she almost jumped out of her skin when Luca's authoritative tone rang out behind her. He was clearly at the end of his rope.

'*Dio!* Why won't you tell me what is wrong? Do I have to stand here in ignorance all morning until you finally decide to explain?'

Tucking her hair behind her ear, Kate struggled with the sudden giant wave of embarrassment that washed over her. Confessing to Luca that she was pregnant was one thing—discussing the intimate facts of that condition with him was entirely another, she was discovering. Especially when he stood there looking so devastatingly gorgeous, and not a little intimidating.

'I had some vaginal bleeding this morning that worried me. I rang my doctor and he told me to go straight to the hospital to have things checked out.'

The tension in Luca's enigmatic features had definitely increased. Something in Kate was genuinely moved and surprised that he seemed to care so much. *At least about the baby...*

'They told me that there's nothing to be alarmed about. Apparently it's very common in the first twelve to fourteen weeks of pregnancy for women to experience some bleeding. But they did an ultrasound scan as an extra precaution.'

'And what did the scan reveal?' Luca all but demanded.

'That everything was fine and the baby is growing perfectly normally inside the womb. The ultrasound can show if a woman is having an ectopic pregnancy, for example—that's when the baby is growing outside the womb.'

'And are you still bleeding now?'

'No.' Kate smiled a little self-consciously. 'I'm absolutely fine.'

Her calm reply belied the sheer panic that had swept over her earlier that morning, when she had gone to the bathroom and discovered the bleed. Until the idea of possibly losing her baby had presented itself, Kate had not fully realised to what extent she truly wanted the child. If her relationship with Luca was destined not to last then at least she would retain the most wonderful gift from their passionate union in which to always remember him.

And she would have someone to love and cherish as her own. The ultrasound had shown her the first pictures of the baby in her womb, and Kate had been both awed and ecstatic at the sight of them. Not to mention emotional. A big part of her had wanted to phone Luca from the hospital and ask him to meet her there. But, unsure as to how he would react, she'd decided against it and asked him to meet her at home instead.

'And you are not in any pain or discomfort?'

'No.'

'We shouldn't have made love last night!'

Seeing the corners of his sensuous mouth tighten in bitter regret, Kate was shocked. 'What?'

'Maybe I was a little too passionate.'

'What happened was nothing to do with us making love, Luca!' Hastening to reassure him, Kate saw straight away that he wasn't going to be easily convinced—and her heart went out to him.

When he lifted his chin, his compelling blue gaze captured her in its dazzling and forceful lights.

'And what did the doctors at the hospital advise you to do now this has happened? Did you tell them that we were just about to fly out to Milan?'

'Yes, I did.'

'And?'

'They told me that it was perfectly okay and to carry on as normal, really. I just need to make sure I don't overdo things and keep physical and mental stress to a minimum—as well as eat sensibly and rest whenever I can.'

'Now I am certain I have made the right decision to take you back to Milan!'

Kate was magnetised by the hypnotic ocean of azure blue that stared back at her with such unarguable authority and intensity.

'The sooner we get away from these shores the better! I cannot guarantee the weather in Milan at this time of year, but I can ensure that when we are there you will have the opportunity to rest and relax properly. I will make sure of it! No doubt you have been under more stress than you realize, Katherine!'

Crossing the room, Luca glanced outside at the now teeming rain and Kate thought she saw him shiver.

'Perhaps…'

'There is no "perhaps" about it!' He shook his head in dismay, and his expression was resolute when he turned back to face her. 'I am very relieved that I got you to stop working when I did! I only hope that the stress you were already under has not had a detrimental effect on the child. I personally do not want to take the risk that anything else might go wrong, so when we get to Milan I will arrange an appointment for you with a top obstetrician and gynaecologist to make sure everything is absolutely as it should be with your pregnancy. In my view it makes absolute sense to get a second opinion, and you can rest assured we will be taking no more chances where this baby *or* yourself is concerned!'

'You sound as if you finally believe that the baby is yours.'

The statement was out of Kate's mouth before she realised. The man who dominated her suddenly inadequate front room with his imposing presence and arresting good looks did not flinch—but he gazed at her with a glance that was unwavering and direct.

'I do.'

'What—what changed your mind?'

'Last night.' Those impressively broad shoulders of his lifted in a tense little shrug, as if his short comment needed no further explanation.

Kate's blood zinged with hope. Suddenly she found that the prospect of going to Milan with Luca was not so daunting, and after the worrying scare she had had this morning a holiday was growing more and more appealing by the minute. It would also be a perfect opportunity for him to get to know her and for her to get to know him. Maybe if they spent some proper time together he would begin to see that she really *was* a woman he could trust. A woman who would fight tooth and nail to protect and take care of the people she loved and would never betray them! To have a family of her own was all she'd ever dreamed of. All Kate needed was a chance.

'Will we still fly out to Italy today?' she asked.

Checking the time on his watch, Luca nodded. 'I rang the airfield just before I arrived here. They have managed to give us another couple of hours before we need to be there. Have you packed yet?'

'I made a start late last night, but because of what happened this morning I've still some to do.'

'Then why don't you go and carry on with it now? As soon as you are finished we will drive to the airfield.'

Feeling suddenly weary, as well as relieved that the planned trip was still going ahead, Kate nodded. 'Okay. Sit down and make yourself at home while you wait for me.'

'Do you need any help? I do not want you over-doing things.'

'I'll be fine.'

'Why do I get the feeling you have been saying that for a long time, Katherine? *Too* long, perhaps?'

Smiling awkwardly, Kate moved to leave the room before she gave way to the tears that were already stinging the backs of her lids and threatening to fall. She'd had a genuine shock and it was only hitting her now.

'Katherine?'

For the most knee-trembling moment, as Luca walked towards her, Kate thought he was going to kiss her. The idea of him holding her close and being tender with her was heavenly. She realised she'd been craving just that since the moment she'd seen him waiting on the doorstep.

'What is it?' She dashed away a tear with the back of her hand.

'This is the right thing we are doing…going to Milan. I do not want you to worry about a thing. It will all be all right, little one.'

As if trying to control the impulse to be closer to her, for reasons known only to himself, Luca gently grazed the back of his hand across her cheek instead of drawing her into his arms, and Kate could not deny she was bitterly disappointed.

'I'd better get on with my packing.' This time she moved with real purpose, and closed the door swiftly behind her….

* * *

During the flight to a private airfield near Milan Luca had barely been able to take his eyes off Katherine. She had dozed for most of the journey, but that had hardly reassured him. Ever since he had learned of the scare she had had that morning his stomach had been twisted with knots that yanked harder and harder, and filled him with a stark, cold terror that she might lose the baby.

Could fate really be so pitiless as to allow him to build up his hopes for a child—only for those hopes to be cruelly crushed all over again?

And what of the effect losing the baby would have on Katherine herself? Luca was certain her attempts to convince him everything was all right hid a genuine fear that it might not be. His instincts were naturally to offer her some comfort, but this thing that sometimes overtook them both knew no bounds—and surely after the scare she had had they had to be careful? That was why he had not followed through on his impulse to take her into his arms when she came back from the hospital. He was genuinely fearful that his desire for her might again consume and overwhelm him.

Sighing inwardly, Luca shook his head. Sometimes he sensed such strength in this fascinating woman. She could give as good as she got, certainly. But at other times there was a fragility there that made him see that Katherine was vulnerable too. And finding out that she was pregnant by a man she'd shared only one passionate night with in a foreign country—a man she knew nothing about—must have made her feel intensely vulnerable and scared, given her history. Even more so after the situation she had described with her faithless ex-fiancé.

Where before Luca had had to wrestle with feelings of anger and jealousy at the thought of her being with another man after she'd left him that morning in Milan, now new sensations were definitely taking over where she was concerned. And if he chose not to scrutinise those sensations too closely, then he told himself he had the right—given his own tumultous past. *Undoubtedly there was still a great need in him to protect himself.* But what was becoming only too clear to him also was that Katherine was now *his* responsibility, and he had a duty to look after her. The coming baby sealed that incontrovertible fact! So…not only would he be insisting that she move in with him permanently while they were away, but just as soon as Luca could arrange it she would become the next Mrs De Rossi. Whether that suited her plans or not!

CHAPTER EIGHT

LUCA had left Kate alone in the sumptuous bedroom where he had first made love to her all those months ago to unpack. The memories of that night submerged her, and filled her with feelings that she barely knew what to do with. Erotic, but also tender, loving feelings. *They had conceived their baby in this amazing Emperor-sized bed with its luxurious satin counterpane and silk cushions...*

Catching her breath as she smoothed her hand over the lush materials, Kate breathed out deeply. One thing was for sure. She was relieved to find out that they would be sharing a bed!

It had definitely disturbed her that since her scare that morning Luca had seemed to somehow distance himself from her a little bit. *Almost as if he was wary of touching her.* Yet at the same time his gaze followed her, as though he was fearful she might suddenly have taken ill and…worse…lose the baby. If only he would talk to her about his fears! Then she might be able to allay them. But talking might lead to his becoming closer to Kate emotionally, and she guessed instinctively that Luca was definitely still keeping his guard up where emotions were concerned.

What had happened to make him so guarded? Had there been a woman in his past who had left him or treated him badly, perhaps? If they shared a bed together, maybe intimacy would give Kate the chance to try and get past some of those high walls Luca seemed to surround himself with. She smiled wryly at herself. Frankly it amazed her that she was thinking on such lines. She had, after all, vowed she would never trust another man again after what had happened in the not too distant past. But knowing that she was going to have Luca's baby and being with him again was slowly changing all that.

Firmly returning her focus to the present, Kate mused how strange it was to be back in this magnificent house…particularly in this room. The setting was familiar, yet it was almost like a scene from a dream. Her heart skipped a beat and a fierce longing for Luca arrowed straight to her womb. With a soft gasp she laid her hand on the gently rounded swell of her stomach, as if to reassure both herself *and* the baby that everything would be all right. Somehow they would find a way.

If she was brave enough to reach out to Luca and stop feeling so insecure perhaps he would also take a risk and open his heart to her as she yearned for him to do? He must need love as much as she did, she was sure. If something in his past had hurt him and left him emotionally scarred then Kate wanted to know about it. Once or twice she'd seen the shadows of an encounter so painful and disturbing in his sky-blue gaze that she'd wanted to hold on to him and never let him go. *In those moments she would have traded every bit of insecurity and fear of rejection to comfort him.*

Hugging herself, she glanced round at the magnificent art on the walls, at the exquisite furnishings that enhanced the room's elegant Italianate beauty, and couldn't help but feel confronted with the wealth and experience that made Luca's everyday existence so distant from hers. Such a confrontation easily provoked old and unhelpful feelings of not being quite good enough. But Kate couldn't let them sabotage the hope she'd started to nurture in her heart that she and Luca might have a real future together.

Squaring her shoulders, she determinedly willed away the discomfort. If Luca didn't want to be with her, she silently contested, then he would hardly have brought her to Milan with him, would he?

'*Buongiorno*, Signorina Richardson!'

A smiling, full-figured woman with threads of iron-grey in her black hair, wearing a white apron over a charcoal-grey dress, approached Kate as she reached the bottom of the elegant winding staircase. She extended her hand in greeting.

'I am Orsetta Leoni—Signor De Rossi's housekeeper. I have been with his family for a very long time, and since they are all sadly gone…now I just look after him! I am very pleased to meet you, Signorina Richardson.'

Her smile was engaging, and as Kate put her hand in hers she silently acknowledged that it was very pleasant to be greeted so warmly. But she was anxious too. She'd waited so long for Luca to return to their bedroom that she'd worried he must have forgotten she was there! As lovely as the beautiful room was, she had wanted to go out on the terrace and sample some of the surprisingly warm, blossom-scented afternoon air.

'*Buongiorno*.' Kate smiled back. 'It's very nice

to meet you too. I was just wondering if you could tell me where I can find Signor De Rossi?'

'*Sì!* Of course! Follow me, Signorina Richardson. I will take you to him.'

Reaching the opened French windows that led out from the drawing room onto the large, fragrantly scented stone terrace, with its bushes of pink and white camellia starting to bloom, Orsetta dropped her hands to her ample hips and tutted.

'He works too hard! I am always telling him!' she announced. 'His *mamma* would turn in her grave that he does not look after himself better!'

Kate's surprised gaze fell upon Luca's sleeping form, stretched out on a rattan sofa. He had removed his jacket, she saw, but was still wearing the suit that he'd worn to travel in. His tie was pulled away from his open collar—as was his habit—and his dark hair flopped boyishly onto his tanned brow. Kate mused that he looked like a delectable male equivalent of the Sleeping Beauty. But Orsetta's words about him not taking better care of himself had wrung at her heart, and she turned briefly to the older woman in acknowledgement.

'You're right. He does work too hard,' she agreed.

'Go and sit down, *signorina*. I will bring you something nice to drink. Some fruit juice, perhaps?'

'That would be lovely…*grazie.*'

Gazing out over lush green gardens, with the rooftops of the city clearly visible in the distance, Kate sighed with pleasure at the warm kiss of the sun on her face. *Luca might not have been able to guarantee constant sunshine at this time of year, but it was certainly far warmer than she had expected.*

Rising to her feet, she removed the light pink cotton cardigan she wore over a navy linen dress, spreading it over the back of her chair. As she did so Luca stirred, murmuring something in his sleep, and once again Kate's glance was riveted by him. Unable to help herself, she moved nearer to better appreciate the full wondrous sight that was Gianluca De Rossi. He was so handsome, with those beautiful carved features and sweeping dark lashes, that she was certain he must have driven all the girls crazy even as a young boy.

Suddenly something disturbed his outwardly relaxed sleep. He grimaced as though in pain, jerking his head to the side, and a film of sweat broke out on his brow. Alarmed, Kate dropped down onto the edge of the rattan sofa and reached for his hand to comfort him.

'It's all right…it's all right,' she soothed, keeping her voice low. 'I'm here, Luca.'

'Sophia!' he shouted, and gripped on to Kate's hand with what felt like every ounce of his impressive strength.

She sucked in her breath as dizzying pain seared through her arm, but she did not try to break free from his hold. In the back of her mind she thought waking him suddenly might be dangerous. *But who was Sophia?* With her heart pounding fit to burst, she stared in mute shock as a single tear slid out from beneath his luxurious lashes and rolled slowly down his cheek. His eyelids opened, and even the sky at its most bewitching had never looked so heavenly blue.

'You were dreaming.' There was such a catch in Kate's throat that she could barely get the words out. When Luca had cried out her heart had been rent almost in two.

Staring first into her face, then down at her hand, where he still imprisoned it, he blinked with the stunned expression of one desperately trying to disentangle himself from the throes of a deeply troubled sleep. 'I was?'

'Luca…do you think you could let go of my hand, please? You're crushing it.'

'I did not realise.' Abruptly releasing her, he moved dazedly into a sitting position. His fingers scrubbed his cheeks, obliterating all trace of that shocking tear, then pressed into his brow as if to banish the lingering traces of his disturbing dream. 'Forgive me…I did not know what I was doing. Are you all right?'

'I'm fine.'

She didn't care about the pain in her hand and arm. All Kate cared about right then was what had caused Luca to cry out like that and…incredibly… put tears in his eyes.

'You shouted out in your sleep.'

'I was afraid of that.'

'You called out a woman's name…Sophia. Who is she, Luca?'

Laying his hand against his chest, he rubbed it a couple of times beneath the fine cotton of his shirt, as if to soothe a spasm, and then exhaled deeply. 'She was my wife,' he replied.

'Your *wife*?' Suddenly Kate's lips had turned so numb she wondered how she'd managed to move them to speak at all.

'*Sì…*'

'I—I didn't know you'd been married… What happened? Were you divorced?'

'No. She died…drowned.'

Drowned? Deepening shock and horror sifted through Kate's insides. After finally learning what had put those painful shadows behind Luca's eyes, she was filled with a desperate need to comfort and hold him. In that instant it didn't matter to her that he had been married, or even that his wife might have been the love of his life. *Kate only knew at that moment that she was deeply and irrevocably in love with him.* And a fervent hope had begun to burn inside her that perhaps—with the advent of their baby—she could help him see that their future looked much brighter than their pasts?

'What a dreadful thing to happen! Oh, Luca, I'm so sorry!'

She caught his hand and wrapped her palm round it. For long moments he just stared down at their joined hands, and then suddenly *he* was the one in command, lifting Kate's arm closer, to examine the reddening skin round her wrist and further up, near her elbow.

'I hurt you.' His voice was throaty and warm and full of regret.

'You didn't mean to.'

It seemed as if her heart was so full right then that she felt a burning need to declare out loud that she loved him. How would Luca react to such news when his own heart was still clearly full of sorrow for his deceased wife?

'How long ago did Sophia die?' she made herself ask.

Slowly he lowered Kate's arm. 'Just over three years ago.'

'Is that why you seem to put everything into your work—and why you haven't taken a break when you've needed to? Because it helps you stop dwelling on what happened?'

'Perhaps.'

'It must have been a terrible time for you.'

'Some events defy description. You wonder how you survive them…how you keep breathing…but you do.'

'How did it—how did it happen?'

Kate sensed the change in him even before he replied—understood the deep reluctance and the need to self-protect that made him wary of discussing such a painful episode in his life, even if she yearned for him to do just that.

'Not now, Katherine.' He grimaced slightly. 'It is much too pleasant an afternoon to dwell on such things! If we are lucky, the fine weather may last into the evening. I will ask Orsetta to prepare us something special for our dinner, and perhaps we can enjoy it out here on the terrace? Would you like that?'

Swallowing down her disappointment that Luca

was clearly not going to confide in her any further, Kate made herself smile to hide her hurt. 'That sounds lovely,' she agreed.

'And you are quite recovered from the flight over? You slept practically all the way.'

'I'm sorry I was such a dull travelling companion…but I think the events of the morning finally caught up with me. The flight was amazing, though! It's not every day a girl gets the chance to travel in a private jet!'

'And how are you feeling physically? You are not in any pain or discomfort after this morning?'

'Honestly—I'm fine,' Kate told him truthfully, her dark eyes examining the face that had become so dear to her.

'That is good. Tomorrow I will arrange an appointment for you with a specialist in these matters. The sooner you are given a clean bill of health from someone whose judgement I trust, the better I will like it. And then we will be able to relax!'

Whilst she appreciated Luca's obvious concern about her pregnancy, Kate was anxious to ask him about Sophia, and find out a bit more about the woman who had been his wife. It might give her a clue as to his feelings about having someone new in his life. Specifically discover if he was open to loving someone else. Someone like *her*? And what Kate was hoping for, too, was a way of somehow reaching into that clearly wounded heart of his and helping to bring about some healing....

CHAPTER NINE

As Luca dressed for dinner that night, disturbing
threads of the dream he had had about Sophia clung
mercilessly to him. Had bringing Katherine here
made him dream about the wife he had lost? He
hadn't dreamed about her for months now. Was guilt
at the bottom of it? Guilt that he still had a future
to look forward to while she did not?

Staring into his own morose gaze in the full-
length mirror in his dressing room, Luca could not
prevent the unhappy tide of memories that washed
over him. The last few weeks of his wife's life had
been the most difficult of their entire marriage, and
there had been many despairing moments when he
had seriously considered asking her for a divorce.
*Only the pain and accusation in her eyes every time
she looked at him had stopped him.* He hadn't been
able to give her what she most wanted and she'd

blamed him for it. Therefore didn't he deserve to suffer? When she had discovered the reason for her inability to conceive lay with her, instead of helping to build a bridge between them for some healing to come about she had simply withdrawn almost entirely, to a place where Luca hadn't been able to reach her… Where he had increasingly believed she did not *want* him to reach her… *She had shut him out and there hadn't been much that he could do about it.*

At the time he had truly mourned the demise of their once loving relationship, but lately he had found himself wondering whether—if Sophia had lived—he would still be with her now. What future could he have had with a woman whose heart was full of blame and regret? A woman whose whole source of happiness had been tied up with the idea of a baby, and who had withdrawn emotionally, mentally and physically from him as soon as she knew she could not conceive?

Before Luca even realised it, the already fading recollection of Sophia's features was replaced by Katherine's in his mind. Genuine warmth and pleasure spread through him when he thought of her waiting out on the terrace, and powerful anticipation arose at the idea of having her all to himself in the house that he truly considered *home*. His mood began to shift from being morose to a feeling of quiet but undeniable excitement. When she had comforted him after his disturbing dream, he recalled, her beautiful dark eyes had seemed to convey a care and regard that touched him deeply. Struck by the thought, Luca stared harder at his reflection in the mirror, as if for the first time seeing past the pain he carried to the possibility of transforming his life his into something potentially far more hopeful and rewarding.

In deference to the warm evening, Katherine wore her favourite summer dress. It was of peach-coloured linen in a tunic style, with flattering slits at either side of the knee-length hem—a sexy little detail that showed off her firm, shapely legs. Usually she cinched her slender waist with a wide black belt, but—given that she was pregnant, and the soft curve of her belly was getting more defined each day—she had decided to forgo the belt and leave the tunic loose instead.

Sitting out on the terrace, beneath the vine-covered pergola where Orsetta had laid the table in readiness for their meal, she sipped at her glass of sparkling mineral water and waited for Luca to join her. Just the thought of him made her insides flutter nervously.

When he appeared, looking rested and gorgeous after his shower, and dressed in a casual but stylish pair of fawn-coloured trousers and a white linen shirt, Kate knew with certainty that a deep and profound longing was growing inside her to make a truly bonding connection with him that would last a lifetime.

'Orsetta is convinced we have brought the good weather with us!' he teased, slipping into the chair opposite Kate's. 'She tells me that it has been raining every day for almost two weeks now, and did not stop until yesterday evening!'

'She believes in signs and omens, then?'

'Yes…why not?' The broad shoulders beneath the white linen shirt lifted in a nonchalant shrug.

'And do you think our unexpected meeting in your office—when I had no idea it was *you* I had come to work for—could be considered a *good* omen?' Kate speculated, her heart hammering as she surveyed him.

'I hope so.' Luca smiled.

His reply seemed to lack conviction, and disappointment sat like a stone on her chest.

'By the way, you look very beautiful tonight,' he added, the force of his sky-blue glance burning her like little wisps of carnal flame licking across her body.

Struggling to contain the shockingly intimate heat that flooded her, Kate had to draw on every ounce of willpower she owned not to let his disturbing gaze distract her and throw her off track. 'I hope that you—that you have no regrets about bringing me here, Luca?' she commented.

'What do you mean?'

'Well…after what happened earlier. You seemed so upset…that's all. I wondered if you might be having second thoughts?'

'Because of my dream?'

'Yes. You were dreaming about your wife, Luca. The wife you obviously once lived with here. I thought you might—might resent another woman being here instead of her.'

'Well, your conclusion is a wrong one!' He tore his glance away for a moment and stared down hard at the table, as if trying to bring whatever fierce emotion had surfaced inside him under strict control. 'What happened is all in the past, and that is where it should stay! Besides…I would rather not think about that part of my life tonight. I have something important to ask you, Katherine.'

'Something important?' Kate echoed, all her thoughts nervously suspended.

'*Sì*. I think we should get married. I believe it is the right thing to do, under the circumstances.'

'The right thing…?'

'Yes. I would like you to be my wife, Katherine… will you agree?' His previous emotions tightly corralled, there was no sign at all on Luca's arrestingly handsome face of what he was feeling.

In contrast, Kate knew she hadn't a *hope* of disguising what she was feeling…nor did she want to! Apart from her initial elation at Luca's proposal, confusion and not a *little* anger also pulsed through her.

'What you mean is that you think we should get married purely because of the baby.' Her hands clenched tightly round the wrought-iron arms of her chair.

'Not *purely* because of the baby. I do believe we have something between us worth building on, Katherine…do you not agree?'

'Something worth building on?' It sounded as though he were talking about one of his upcoming projects at work, and it wasn't what Kate had hoped to hear at all!

'Besides…' He shrugged, as though not quite sure what to make of her indignation. 'Is it not an honourable enough reason that I should ask you to be my wife because you are expecting my child?'

'Forget honour for a moment! Let's be *real* here, shall we?' Her heart pounding, Kate held her hands in her lap to still their sudden trembling. 'You're asking me to marry you as if my feelings about it hardly matter at all! I'm not just a receptacle for a baby, you know! I'm a woman too! A woman with hopes and dreams that might involve something a little bit deeper than a practical marriage of convenience! How am I supposed to raise a child with you, Luca, when you clearly intend keeping me at a distance? Emotionally, at least! You won't even talk to me about the things in your life that have shaped you or hurt you. Like your wife, for instance. You told me the most shocking thing this afternoon...that she drowned. But when I asked you wouldn't even tell me how it happened! You completely shut down about it and clearly shut *me* out! Whilst I understand that you don't want to keep revisiting the pain and torment you must have gone through, how can you contemplate marrying someone else if you won't at least share something of what happened with them? That's how we get to know each other in a relationship—by sharing our sorrows, joys, hopes and dreams, not just sleeping together!'

Looking as stunned by her outburst as though he had just survived some force of nature that had been unexpectedly unleashed, Luca exhaled a long, slow breath and moved his head from side to side.

Unlinking her hands, Kate forlornly realised she had no hope of keeping them from trembling. *None!* There was simply too much at stake here to remain calm. Luca still hadn't spoken. Unhappily believing that he obviously wasn't going to answer any of her highly charged questions, Kate felt hope die inside her. She felt like crying.

But then, with the tension around his sensual mouth lessening just a fraction, surprisingly he seemed to change his mind. 'We were holidaying with some friends on their yacht on the southern coast…Amalfi, to be precise.'

Her attention irrevocably captured, Kate relaxed against the back of chair, her hands resting protectively over her stomach.

'Sophia was relaxing on one of the sun decks and told me she just wanted to read her book and try and take her mind off things.' Looking straight into Kate's transfixed gaze, Luca swallowed hard. 'We had been through a difficult time…a *very* difficult time. For three years we had been trying for a baby, without success. In the last of those three years we decided to have some investigations done as to why we could not conceive a child. We found out that there was a problem with Sophia's ovaries that could not be rectified and that pregnancy was impossible. She was devastated.

'From when we were first together we had always known we wanted a family. I was my parents' only child, and they had both died by the time I was twenty-one. I wanted to fill this beautiful villa they had left me with the sound of my children's laughter…many children! Sophia was one of six girls, and had had a brother who died. Because of that she dreamed about giving her parents a boy grandchild. All we had seemed to talk about…hope for…dream of…for three long years was having a baby! I told her that we could adopt now we could not have one of our own…that I was happy to do that. I meant it. But Sophia was *not* happy. Every day she was in tears. Then more and more she retreated inside herself, and eventually she would barely talk to me about how she felt at all.

'That morning, about half an hour after I had left her relaxing on the sun deck, I returned to see how she was and found her chair empty and her book left open at the page she was reading beside it. Thinking she might have gone to lie down in the cabin, I searched for her. But, no…there was no sign. Unable to ignore the sense of fear that was building in me, I ran to find my friends and we all searched the boat together.'

Frowning deeply at the memory, his jaw tight, Luca took a couple of moments before continuing. 'Her body was found later on that afternoon by the coastguard. There were railings around the deck where she had been sitting. There was no way she could have just fallen overboard. After a full investigation by the police the coroner returned a verdict of death by suicide.'

Scrubbing a hand round his jaw, Luca stared hard at Kate. 'What I want to know…what has been eating me up inside for over three years…is did I help drive Sophia to take her own life by my great desire to be a father? Did I put too much pressure on her when as it turns out she was so fragile?'

'Oh, Luca! It doesn't sound remotely to me as if that's what happened at all!' Her heart pierced by the way Luca's wife had died, as well as by the raw pain in his voice as he confessed what had been troubling him the most about her death, Kate leaned across the table and reached for his hand. 'From what you've told me, Sophia wanted children as much as you—maybe more! For some women it can take over their lives…the desire to have a baby. I had a friend it affected in that way. She had a wonderful marriage, a loving, caring husband, but she just couldn't get pregnant. In the end, because of the obsession that consumed her, the marriage broke up. I met her husband a while afterwards, and he told me that he'd had to leave because he had started to feel as though he'd ceased to exist. My friend cared more about having a baby than him! In a relationship you have to take care of each other too…don't you think?'

Smiling gently, Kate clasped Luca's hand in both of hers.

'For whatever reason, Sophia did what she did. It sounds like her deep personal sorrow went *beyond* where anybody could reach her or help her put it right. Not even a loving husband! I'm sorry for what you both must have endured in not being able to have a child of your own. But I'm more sorry for what *you* have had to endure since—blaming yourself for Sophia's tragic death.'

Luca did not know what to say. All he knew was that the kindness that shone like a fiercely bright beacon from Katherine's beguiling gaze was stirring him in the most profound way. It was making him dare to imagine that life could be far better than it had been for a long time, and he realised that he passionately wanted that. *You have to take care of each other too*, she had reminded him. Well…he could definitely relate to Katherine's friend's husband. Sophia had hardly even *looked* at him in the final weeks of her life, when her sorrow over not being able to conceive a child had made her withdraw further and further inside herself.

It was not until now that Luca had fully allowed himself to experience the reality of feeling both rejected and neglected by her. There had been times when he had been so alone with the deep unhappiness that racked him that he'd hardly been able to bear it! And for the past three years he had shut out every bit of possible comfort from another human being in order to protect himself from any further hurt. It was as though he had hidden himself in a deep dark cave when he had really needed to place himself in the light…in the warmth…in a place where he could see that life *did* have more to offer than just more pain.

What if Katherine was that place Luca needed to be?

'I would like something,' he said now, getting to his feet and coaxing her to hers. Holding her hands, he sensed her sweet, lovely scent dance on the warm air between them, and it stirred into life the deep, exquisite longing that had become his constant companion since that very first time Luca had laid eyes on her.

'Anything,' she replied softly, her delectable dark brown eyes shimmering.

'A kiss,' he breathed, and, gently sliding his fingers beneath her delicate jaw, he drew her face towards his own.

Their lips met and clung, the heartfelt contact instigating a renewed vitality and a sense of coming home that moved Luca almost unbearably. The longing inside him grew into a sharp hunger as their tongues mingled and danced, and glorious wild honey infiltrated his bloodstream, banishing all previous traces of sorrow from his mind. All he wanted to do was gather Katherine up into his arms and carry her through the mansion's high, echoing corridors to their bedroom, then make love to her long into the fragrant moonlit evening.

But just when Luca had decided to act on that feverish, irresistible impulse, he remembered her visit to the hospital, and the reason he had made the decision to bring her to Milan. *He would not jeopardise either Katherine's wellbeing or the baby's because he could not control his near overwhelming desire for her!* To deny himself what he craved above all else was pure torture, but Luca had to heed the logic of his own reasoning.

Gradually, and reluctantly, he began to ease out

of the sweetly erotic kiss that promised to lead to so much more if he would just let it. Sensing the tension in Katherine's slender frame, and cupping her face, letting the luxurious curtain of sable hair ripple onto her shoulders, Luca stroked his thumbs across her impossibly soft cheeks and smiled. 'You kiss like an angel. You could make any man your slave with such kisses!'

'But I don't want just "any" man, Luca.'

'No?' he teased. The promise in her eyes could not help but increase the powerful need that already gripped him, and it made his body ache for her so much that Luca could have wept with frustration.

'Don't you know?' she asked. 'Don't you know how much I—'

'*Scusi*, Signor De Rossi…*signorina*…'

Luca's smiling housekeeper appeared. She was carrying some drinks on a small round tray which she placed on the pretty lattice work iron table beside them. Inwardly cursing at the interruption—what had Katherine been going to say to him just then?—Luca glanced wryly at the woman whose lovely face he still framed between his hands and reluctantly allowed her to extricate herself and move away.

He made a joke in Italian to Orsetta about her unfortunate timing and the older woman swiftly apologised, glancing over at Katherine with an apologetic shrug of the shoulders. Luca found he did not have it in him to be angry with this most faithful and loyal member of his staff. Instead he thanked her for her thoughtfulness in bringing them refreshments. Beaming at him, Orsetta told him that dinner would not be long, then left him and Katherine alone again.

'That night when we first met...you told me you felt lost.' She had moved back to her seat at the table and was frowning up at him as she spoke. 'Was that because you were thinking about your wife?'

What was she getting at? Luca wondered. He went up behind her and laid his hands on her shoulders. With a primal satisfaction he felt the definite quiver that rippled through her in response to his touch.

'She had been on my mind that day, yes,' he admitted. 'But only because I had inadvertently found the book she had been reading on the yacht. Of course it had stirred things up inside me. But can we not talk about this any more tonight? I would much rather concentrate on us!'

'All right, then.'

'Now...where were we before Orsetta interrupted us? Ah, yes... You were also about to tell me something? What was it, Katherine?'

'Do you know what?' She turned towards him,

her expression guarded all of a sudden, her eyes only briefly meeting his, as if she feared Luca might see something she did not want him to see. 'Could we talk about this later? I suddenly feel the need to go and lie down for a while. The effect of all the travelling has definitely caught up with me. Do you mind if I give dinner a miss tonight? I'm really not hungry at all.'

'It is not a question of if I mind, Katherine! Are you feeling all right? You are not unwell?' Luca's voice was unwittingly sharp as he misread the reason why Katherine would not look directly at him. He was praying hard she was not trying to conceal some acute discomfort from him that had to do with the baby.

'I'm perfectly well. I'm just a little tired, that's all.'

'You are sure that is all? You are not hiding anything from me?'

'No, Luca. I'm not.'

Disappointed that he could not keep her right where she was, Luca bit back intense frustration and regret. 'Then go and get some rest and I will look in on you later.'

'You really don't mind?'

'Of course not! Why should I object to you going to lie down when I brought you here so that you could have all the rest you need?'

'I'll see you later, then.'

Rising to her feet, Katherine hurried from the terrace. The minute she had gone, and he was alone again, Luca missed her like a limb that had been severed from his body....

CHAPTER TEN

WAS Luca still in love with his wife? When he had
admitted that he had been thinking about her the
night they had met, Kate's heart had sunk with new
hurt. Could his continuing sorrow over her death
have driven him into Kate's arms that night? He had
asked her if she had gone to bed with him on the
rebound, but what if he had made love to her purely
because he'd been in need of some physical consolation and nothing else? Had she simply imagined
the strong connection she was so certain she'd felt?

Her mind and body suffused with hurt and confusion, Kate crossed her arms over her chest and
moved towards the open French windows in the
bedroom. Even the heady, sensual scent of lillies
and blossoming mimosa borne on the warm
Mediterranean air could not lift her spirits right
then. Staring out unseeingly, she shook her head.

Luca had suggested they marry, but what hope had she for a future with him if his heart still belonged to a woman who no longer lived? she asked herself. And how would their child fare growing up in such an atmosphere?

On the terrace just now—before his housekeeper had appeared—Kate had been going to confess that she loved him, but the moment had passed and she had lost the courage to pursue it.

Moving over to the enormous bed, she picked up a satin pillow and clutched it to her chest, then dropped down onto the lush counterpane. *What should she do?*

'Katherine?'

She glanced up in astonishment to find the object of her musing at the door. Closing it behind him, Luca walked towards her. *He owned the room with that walk...* He would captivate any woman in any room anywhere with just the sheer magnetism of his presence, Kate was certain. There would always be a ripple of excitement...of danger...a need to discover what made such an enigmatic man tick... followed by a silent gnawing hunger to know what it would feel like to be made love to by him.

Kate knew that because they were exactly the sensations *she* had experienced when she had seen him for the first time. And that same dizzying leap of hunger and pleasure and bone-melting desire sizzled through her now. Practically on sight she had detected that that there was something behind that civilised Mediterranean façade of his that hinted at a certain wildness of spirit—of nature—underneath. But, although he had more than his fair share of arresting masculine attributes, there was also a grace about Gianluca De Rossi that made him even more spellbinding and unforgettable in Kate's eyes.

'What is it? Is something the matter?'

'No.' As Luca reached the side of the bed, the expression on his handsome face was both reflective and brooding as he gazed down at her. 'Yes. As a matter of fact there *is* something the matter.'

Swallowing hard, Kate stared, her mind racing towards all kinds of distressing conclusions. The main one being that he didn't want her with him after all. *He was still in love with the memory of his wife.*

'I want to know what you were going to tell me just now…when we were out on the terrace. I could not relax when you left because the words you had started to say kept going round and round in my head and I will not have any peace until I know!'

Clutching the crimson cushion against her chest even more tightly, Kate widened her dark eyes as she gazed up at Luca. Backed into a corner, she could either prevaricate or simply speak the truth. *She chose the latter.*

'I was going to say…don't you know how much I love you?'

Someone exhaled…deeply. She did not know whether it was him or her. The sound brushed through the air like velvet.

'You love me?' he asked.

'Yes…I do.'

Because she detected no immediate change in Luca's serious façade, Kate was gripped by such a terrible cold fear that he was about to reject her that all her faculties seemed to suddenly freeze. But then he started to smile, and again she was struck by how hypnotic that blue-eyed gaze of his could be…how *lethal* to someone who had found she had no defences at all to protect herself from an expression that struck the most profound, unmatched delight in her heart and made her more vulnerable than she'd ever been in her life.

'That is all right, then.'

'It is?'

'*Sì*. Now I can relax, *tesoro mio*.'

Before Kate realised his intention, Luca had dropped down onto the bed beside her and was stroking his hand over her hair. She heard the muted thud of his shoes hit the carpet as he kicked them off and her body quivered almost violently.

'You don't mind?' she whispered. 'That I love you?'

He chuckled, and the deliciously sensual sound was like being wrapped in the most luxurious warm towels after a deep, fragrant, longed-for hot bath.

'Do you know what it is like for a man who has more or less given up on the possibility of happiness for ever to hear a woman he cares for deeply say that she loves him?' His hand swept her hair back from her face and tenderly cupped her cheek. 'I fell in love with you the night of the party, my dear Katherine. This is true. It was a party that I did not want to give…but by the end of the evening I was glad that I had—because I met *you*.'

'And you're not still in love with your wife, Luca? From time to time when you seemed to hold back from me I thought it was because of that!'

'If I did hold back it was because I did not want to overwhelm you with my desire for you…nor potentially harm the baby! When you had that scare this morning, before we flew out to Milan, I was devastated at the thought that something might happen to you or our unborn child! Listen to me

Katherine. I know my own heart and it belongs to you now…not to poor Sophia! It was a terrible tragedy that she died the way she did, but it is *you* I love! You need never fear that I am lying about that!'

'All this time?' She pulled his hand away from her face and held it. 'You've loved me all this time, Luca?'

'*Sì.*'

His gorgeous smile, delicious voice and incredible eyes all made Kate feel weak…deliriously, happily weak.

'But when you left like you did the next morning I was thrown into confusion! My pride was hurt too, so I did not try to find you. Then three months later you miraculously appear, only for me to learn that our night together had resulted in you falling pregnant! And it seemed to me that you had made no effort in all that time to even let me know! For a while I confess that I had the most terrible suspicions that the baby might not be mine. I will tell you now that I was tormented by the very idea that you had been with another man after the incredible night we had shared!'

'I made you miserable.' Kate's sigh was heavy with regret. 'But I didn't mean to. I really *did* want to get in touch with you, Luca, but I was petrified of making another mistake after what had happened to me before…when my ex did what he did… That night stirred up a lot of painful stuff from my past…difficult and hurtful memories that really stung. Mostly it stirred up my old feelings of not being good enough! That's why I ran away that morning in Milan. I feared that in the cold light of day you would reject me anyway, and therefore I should spare myself the pain and leave you first!'

Gazing into Luca's eyes, she let her slender shoulders slump a little.

'My mother died not long before I got together with Hayden, and my confidence was badly shaken by her death. That's the truth. I think that's why I deluded myself about him. I just wanted somebody to really care about me because I was frightened of being alone. But I could never have gone with another man after being with you, Luca…*never*!'

Levelling his arresting glance on her with serious-ness and concern, Luca entwined his fingers tightly with Kate's as he spoke. 'Hear this. I will never reject you—and neither do I want you ever to feel not good enough again! You have no reason to believe that about yourself, no matter what anyone else says or does! You are a lovely, beguiling woman, and as well as your outer beauty it is the beauty of your soul that touches my heart the most, sweet Katherine.'

Barely knowing how to answer such a wonderful declaration, Kate leaned forward and touched her lips gently to Luca's cheek. The whisper of sandalwood-scented cologne and the soft/rough texture of his skin was a sensual cocktail bar none.

'You don't know what it means to me to hear you say that! And now I have something to show you.'

Leaning across him to reach the cherrywood cabinet beside the bed, Kate retrieved her purse and took out what looked to be a black and white photograph. Handing it to Luca, she tucked her hair behind her ear and smiled.

'This is a picture of our baby in my womb. The hospital gave it to me after I had my ultrasound.'

He was staring down at the photograph as though studying the meaning of the universe. There was the brief movement of a muscle contracting at the corner of his mouth, and Kate saw how affected he was. She had experienced the same mixture of awe and elation when she'd first seen the picture.

'They asked me if I wanted to know the baby's sex but I said no… You don't mind waiting to find out, do you?'

Tearing his gaze away from the photo at last, and raising his head to look at Kate, Luca knew his feelings were transparent. 'I do not mind…no. It will be all the more wonderful on the day of the birth to find out then! This is such a miracle to me—to see this…' He shook his head almost with reverence. 'It is something I thought never to see! God is good, yes?'

'Yes, Luca.' Kate smiled. 'God *is* good. And I know I have many reasons to count my blessings! Why don't you keep the picture in your wallet?'

'I would like that.' He tucked it carefully into his shirt pocket.

'And you won't hold it against me even the smallest bit that I ran away that morning?'

'No…' He appeared to be mulling the idea over. 'But you *will* have to recompense me…and in a way of my choosing.'

'Oh?'

Immediately Kate saw that he was teasing her, and her tummy flipped as her body was suffused with the most delicious heat. He was staring at the row of buttons down the front of her dress, and one by one he started to undo them.

Looking up, he caught and held her startled glance. 'I want to see my woman—the mother of my child—as God made her.'

Letting out a shaky breath, Kate hardly dared move a muscle. Although her need for him was great, she welcomed this unexpectedly gentle side to his lovemaking with a profound pang of love and excitement. The reverence with which he undid her clothing was even more erotic than if he had torn it off her body in a blaze of passionate heat, and she couldn't help shivering.

Removing her dress completely, he laid his hands on the slender slopes of her shoulders and kissed her once, twice on the mouth, then drew deliberately away again when Kate's lips would have clung to his for more. Smiling knowingly, lazily, perfectly aware that he was drawing out the tension between them, playing it like the most exquisite harpstring, Luca was clearly revelling in having the upper hand.

Slowly, as if he were painting a picture, he traced a line with his finger from the base of Kate's throat to the cleft between her breasts. Impending motherhood had changed her body, and she knew with silent satisfaction and a little spurt of pride that for the first time ever she had a cleavage to envy. Stroking his fingers lightly across the fulsome curves of her breasts, Luca let them dip for a moment to press open the front fastening of Kate's lacy pink bra. She held her breath. Exposed to the softly warm scented air, her exquisitely sensitive nipples throbbed and contracted almost sharply. Her teeth came down hard on her lip. Then a helplessly husky groan left her throat as Luca put his mouth to a breast and suckled gently.

The silken cavern of the inside of his mouth and the slide of his tongue over her bared flesh was like ambrosia from the gods. An arrow of heat found its erotic target, deep in her core, and devastatingly ignited. Lifting his head momentarily, Luca gave the same exquisite attention to her other breast, and Kate threaded her fingers through the soft dark strands of his hair and clung on even as she silently, passionately begged for mercy. *Surely this much pleasure couldn't be allowed? Surely it was visited only on the lucky few?*

Hungrily seeking Luca's mouth, she accepted his returning rough, hot kiss with an almost unbearable need to have him even closer. *She wanted him inside her...to have no distinction between her body and his...to be skin to skin, heart to heart, soul to soul...* Her hands all but tore at his clothes, and finally, irresistibly, Luca helped. The erotic game he'd started had given rise to its own wild momentum, and finally they were just reeds, swept away by the powerful rapids that overtook them.

His naked, hard body covering hers, Kate felt her hips soften and her thighs open as Luca's hands caressed and readied her for his possession. Her heart thumped in a primal drumbeat that steadily grew stronger inside her, and, following the perfect taut musculature of his back down to his buttocks, Kate hungrily reacquainted herself with every fascinating facet, slope and curve of the powerful male body.

'I will go as slowly as I can.' Luc smiled ruefully into her eyes as he momentarily stilled above her. 'I do not want to hurt you, *tesoro mio*… You must tell me if you need me to stop at any time.'

Stop? Whilst Kate totally appreciated the love and concern Luca was expressing, she wanted to tell him she might not *live* if he didn't give them both what they so desperately wanted right there and then and not a second later! Reaching up, she drew her finger softly across a mouth that was so sensually beautiful she almost wanted to weep at its sheer artistic perfection.

'You don't have to worry, Luca,' she told him tenderly. 'I'm not made of porcelain and neither is our baby! This is perfectly natural and right and you won't hurt me. Just make love to me…now… *please*…'

To hear Katherine's entreaty for him to make love to her made Luca's heart soar to the heavens. It laid to rest some of the dark ghosts that had haunted him since Sophia had died…that had made him believe he would never know love or happiness with a woman again. Destiny—*and Luca absolutely believed it was indeed destiny*—had brought this lovely woman to his door, and he would be eternally grateful to the universe for its divine intervention. The sight of the ultrasound picture of their baby had made his heart throb with profound joy and gratitude. It had heightened the already powerful emotions he experienced whenever he was with Katherine.

Seeing her sensational sable hair displayed on the pillow behind her now, and with the uninhibited pleasure in her beautiful face as he started to move inside her, he felt proud, possessive and fiercely protective. His whole body was consumed with burning need for her. She had assured him he wouldn't hurt her, but still a part of him was conscious that she carried their growing baby inside her, and so he took extra care not to allow his powerful need to run away with him.

The muscles in his arms straining like corded ropes from his effort to maintain control, Luca relaxed against Katherine a little to stroke his palms over her velvet-soft breasts. They fascinated and enthralled him with their darkened caramel tips, and he filled his hands with their lush fullness.

Giving in to the pure temptation that they wrought, he put his mouth to them again as he drove himself as deep as he dared into Katherine's sweet, hot satin centre. Her skin tasted like the most delicious dessert wine he'd ever sampled, and the evocative, heart-stopping pleasure that drenched him as her scalding heat enfolded him was like a star exploding in its dazzling intensity. It took him to the very brink of his carefully imposed self-control and left him trembling.

'Let go, my love,' Katherine coaxed, her breath warm and silky against his mouth. 'You don't have to wait…let go.'

Her hips thrust upwards to meet Luca's and she wrapped her firm, shapely legs around his waist. He murmured something…he barely knew what…. The intensity of the erotic fire that engulfed him had actually for a moment made him lose his mind. Incredibly, even as he surrendered to Katherine's sensual entreaty, in the same instant Luca felt her tight, hot muscles grip harder around him, then flex and grip again. She gasped, and squeezed her eyelids closed as he pumped urgently into her.

Never before had he and a lover reached the peak of their satisfaction together, at the same time, and the sensations the experience aroused in him were amazing…beyond incredible! He was filled with awe and love for this wonderful woman in his arms. And the thought that they were going to have a child together made Luca's cup of happiness overflow. '*Ti amo… Ti amo,* Katherine!' As he held her face between his hands, every lovely feature she possessed became infinitely dear to him. 'You *have* to agree to be my wife!' he told her passionately. 'Tell me that you will marry me!'

'Yes, Luca… I *will* marry you!'

He frowned. 'I do not take your answer for granted. I want you to be absolutely sure that it is what you want.'

'Did you not hear what I just said?' Now it was Katherine's turn to frown, but her expression was almost instantly replaced by a smile brighter than the Mediterranean sunshine. 'All I know is that I might lose my mind if I *don't* marry you, Luca! Don't you know by now that you're the one I've been waiting for all my life?'

'I am sorry I did not trust you as I should have done when you returned to me! In future I will have no doubt about your loyalty—now I know you love me! So…what would you like from me as a wedding present, hmm?'

Lifting a coil of her lustrous hair and curling it

round his finger, Luca allowed himself to genuinely relax. *If he was the one she had been waiting for all her life, then Luca echoed that statement.* Now he was anxious for them to start married life with a completely fresh page—all past mistakes and misunderstandings erased and wholeheartedly forgiven.

'What about a new house?' he suggested. 'I will design one especially to your taste…here or in London. I do not mind where.'

Katherine appeared momentarily troubled. 'I don't need you to design me a new house, Luca… although the thought is wonderful! I want to fill *this* house with the sound of our children's laughter… just as you said you once longed to do! It is a beautiful house, and I know I will grow to love it. After all…this is the place where we conceived our baby, and it will always be special to me.'

Her sincere words gladdened his heart, and Luca rolled over with Katherine in his arms so that suddenly *she* was the one who had prime position. As her tousled hair fell back into place round her bare shoulders he fastened his hands on either side of her curvaceous hips, positioning her just where he wanted her. He was already more than ready for her again, and she released a surprised but sensual gasp as he deftly slipped inside her moist heat.

'Signor De Rossi!' She waggled her finger at him in mock reprimand. 'You have a way of taking me by surprise that is quite…' she moaned softly '…quite…wonderful!'

'And you, my darling—' Luca grinned back at her '—have the seductive allure of Cleopatra and Botticelli's *Venus* combined! What is a poor man to do but fall at your feet in complete adoration?'

EPILOGUE

Eighteen months later

'I TOLD you once before that you were a very lucky man, Luca, and I say it again now. You are definitely a man other men would envy!' Hassan beamed at Luca as the younger man took a sip of his champagne.

They were standing in one of the swish reception rooms of the Dorchester, where Hassan was throwing a small party to celebrate the completion of the fabulous hotel Luca and his colleagues had designed for him in Dubai. Unfortunately Luca had been unable to fly out to Dubai to the much bigger party he had thrown there, because Luca's wife— the lovely Katherine—was pregnant with their second child and had not been up to flying.

Marriage suited his friend, mused Hassan. There was a kind of contented aura about Luca these days that Hassan had detected more and more during their past few meetings together. He had told Luca that marriage would bring him much contentment and pleasure—but then Katherine De Rossi was a very special woman. *Very* special indeed! Priding himself on being a connoisseur of the fairer sex, and having had the privilege of getting to know her a little since she and Luca had married, Hassan could readily attest to that.

'You will not get an argument from me today about that!' Luca smiled.

'And today you must tell me all about your next project, now that my wonderful hotel is finished!'

'My next project?'

A small buzz of heat ricocheted through Luca as he thought about the next thing he planned to do, after this little gathering came to an end. He was taking a whole month off and spending it with Katherine and his son in Italy. They were flying out to their home in Milan this afternoon, and from there the plan was to do the 'grand tour'—with Luca as guide, of course. He was going to introduce his beloved family to the culture and delights of Rome, Venice, Pisa, and of course Tuscany—where they planned to spend quite a few lazy, sybaritic days soaking up the sunshine and sampling the tempting and delicious foods of the region.

And when little Orlando was asleep at night he and Katherine would make love into the early hours of the morning. *That* particular thought was the main reason for the warmth flowing through Luca's body now.

'My next project is a purely personal one, Hassan,' he informed the older man. 'I'm taking a month off and spending it in Italy with my wife and son.'

'And she is well, the beautiful Katherine?'

'Very well…thank you.'

Luca's mobile phone rang and making his apologies to his friend, he rescued it from his inside jacket pocket, seeing immediately that the call was from the lady in question.

'Ciao, come va?'

*'Bene…*how are you? Enjoying the party?'

Luca was teaching Katherine Italian and she was making good progress…except that she more often than not reverted to English for quickness.

'Mi manchi…' Lowering his voice, Luca smiled, inevitably wanting to be with his wife rather than here, making small talk with a bunch of too-earnest businessmen. But Hassan's business had been good for the De Rossi firm, and his hospitality and friend-

ship were second to none. So Luca would not be churlish about having to spend time with him at a party meant to celebrate their mutual satisfaction and success at the completion of this project.

'I miss you too, and I can't wait to see you so that you can help ease this ache I seemed to have developed in your absence!'

Katherine had replied, and Luca's smile turned into an out-and-out grin. She was a little minx, teasing him like that when he was too far away from her to do anything about it! *Dio!* Was he going to get his own back when he saw her!

'How is Orlando?' he asked, deliberately changing the subject to a far less provocative one—although he did need to hear that everything was okay with his adorable little son.

'Wonderful! I took him for a walk in the park, and right now his nanny is watching over him as he's having his afternoon nap… Which is why I'm waiting for you in the lobby, my darling!'

'You are here? At the hotel?' Luca whispered fiercely, moving even farther away from his friend and clenching his jaw as the small buzz of heat inside him suddenly grew hotter.

'Why don't you come and find me?' Katherine replied teasingly. 'But hurry, because if you're much longer than a couple of minutes I might just change my mind and go home again on my own!'

'*Dio!* Wait and see what will happen to you when I find you! Do not say I did not warn you!'

'I can't wait! I have the most vivid imagination, Luca—you know that… And now you've deliberately put all kinds of delicious ideas into my head!'

'You are killing me—do *you* know that?' He shook his head from side to side in wonderment, in not a little physical discomfort.

'I'm sorry. I know I'm a tease. But I can't help it! I love you so much. And now, with this new baby coming, I love you even more!'

'*Anch'io… Ti amo,* Katerina,' he crooned into the phone, with a brief glance over his shoulder at the almost too patient Hassan, whose beaming smile seemed to be growing ever wider! Luca had pretty much guessed the other man knew who was keeping him so preoccupied on the phone. In fact, he was beginning to suspect that his friend also knew that the lady in question was waiting for him in the lobby!

'Hurry, Luca! I'm waiting…'

Luca returned to where he'd stood before the phone call. 'Katherine has turned up and is waiting for me downstairs…' He started to explain to Hassan, his jaw reddening helplessly.

The older man's smile was as impish as that of a small boy who'd been up to some mischief. 'Yes, I know. We arranged the surprise between us, your delightful wife and I!' he confessed shamelessly.

Luca shook his head. 'You do not mind if I leave the party early?'

'I will make your apologies to everyone. They will understand, seeing as your beautiful wife is pregnant again and needs her husband to be home with her!'

'You are a good friend, Hassan.' Luca shook the other man's hand with not a little haste, his mouth quirking upwards into a conspiratorial grin. 'And I will see you when you are next in London, in a few months… I promise!'

'It has been a pleasure and a delight doing business with you, my friend,' Hassan warmly responded. 'Go well. And do not forget to give my best regards to the exquisite Katherine!'

'What is the meaning of this?'

Feigning a cross expression, Luca stalked across the lobby to where the bewitching brunette in a red silk dress was drawing admiring glances from hotel patrons, as she sat on a leather sofa, rubbing one delightfully shaped stockinged foot, with her discarded high-heeled satin shoe on the floor beside her.

Her expression one of innocence personified, Katherine stared up at Luca as if utterly perplexed as to why he should apparently be so mad at her. 'You took your time!' she scolded him. 'Another minute and I would have jumped in a cab and gone home again!'

Ignoring her completely irrational answer, Luca shook his head and sighed, then sat down beside his wife on the sofa. 'What is the matter? Are your feet hurting again?' he demanded, taking one of the aforementioned feet tenderly between his hands. 'It is your own fault, Katherine! You should be at home, resting, not haring around London like a teenager! You *are* pregnant, remember?'

'Are you saying that I'm too old to be haring around?' she asked sweetly, batting her curling black lashes at him. 'By the way…did you give my love to dear Hassan before you left?'

'I did no such thing!' Luca replied, horrified.

They had been married for a year and a half, but he was still prone to flashes of quick and intense jealousy if Katherine even joked that she found another man remotely attractive—much less told him to pass on her love to one! He knew she did it just to provoke him, and although he was intensely glad to see her now, Luca wished they were at home, so he could quieten her teasing with an afternoon of torrid lovemaking. At least until Orlando woke up from his nap! Perhaps if they hastened home now they could do exactly that?

Anticipation building inside him, Luca sighed. Hassan was perfectly right, of course. Luca *was* a lucky man. The luckiest man in the world as far as he was concerned! After the pain of his past he could never have imagined a future so bright and so full of love. His feelings were *beyond* grateful. 'Katherine?'

'Yes, Luca?'

'You are a little minx, but I love and adore you and our son more than I can ever say!' He stopped rubbing her foot and gave her a quick hard kiss on the lips. As her satisfied sigh feathered over him, Luca grinned. 'And I love the new baby that is coming too! You have given me more love and happiness than I could ever have dreamed of, my angel!'

The teasing disappeared from Katherine's beguiling dark eyes, to be replaced by a serious look. He heard a distinct sniff, and his stomach clenched with concern.

'Katherine?'

'I'm all right, darling. I'm just feeling a little emotional…especially when you say such lovely things to me! It makes me wonder what I've done to deserve all this…you and our beautiful children! I get so scared that it will be taken away from me!'

Glancing back into her lovely face, Luca shook his head. 'Nothing bad is going to happen to any of us, sweetheart. I promise you that! We made a vow not to dwell on the things in the past that hurt us, remember? Instead we will approach every day we are blessed with in confidence and faith. Look, why don't I contact Brian and ask him to meet us out front right now? If we leave soon then maybe we can have some time together before Orlando wakes and we are needed.'

'Shirley is with him, and she won't mind if we make ourselves scarce for a while. She knows how much I've been pining for you!'

Luca's anticipation at getting his beautiful wife alone, for a couple of hours at least, almost made him groan out loud with imagined pleasure. Standing up, he temporarily crouched to slip the black satin shoe back onto her slender foot, then helped Katherine to her feet.

Slipping a possessive arm around her waist, he kissed her again on the mouth. 'I love you, *tesoro mio*!' Luca passionately declared out loud, not caring who heard him. And his declaration was silently followed by a wish that every other man and woman present could experience even an *ounce* of the love he and Katherine felt for each other....

* * * * *

Harlequin offers a romance for every mood!
See below for a sneak peek from our paranormal
romance line, Silhouette® Nocturne™.
Enjoy a preview of REUNION by USA TODAY
bestselling author Lindsay McKenna.

Aella closed her eyes and sensed a distinct shift, like movement from the world around her to the unseen world.

She opened her eyes. And had a slight shock at the man standing ten feet away. He wasn't just any man. Her heart leaped and pounded. He reminded her of a fierce warrior from an ancient civilization. Incan? She wasn't sure but she felt his deep power and masculinity.

I'm Aella. Are you the guardian of this sacred site? she asked, hoping her telepathy was strong.

Fox's entire body soared with joy. Fox struggled to put his personal pleasure aside.

Greetings, Aella. I'm the assistant guardian to

this sacred area. You may call me Fox. How can I be of service to you, Aella? he asked.

I'm searching for a green sphere. A legend says that the Emperor Pachacuti had seven emerald spheres created for the Emerald Key necklace. He had seven of his priestesses and priests travel the world to hide these spheres from evil forces. It is said that when all seven spheres are found, restrung and worn, that Light will return to the Earth. The fourth sphere is here, at your sacred site. Are you aware of it? Aella held her breath. She loved looking at him, especially his sensual mouth. The desire to kiss him came out of nowhere.

Fox was stunned by the request. *I know of the Emerald Key necklace because I served the emperor at the time it was created. However, I did not realize that one of the spheres is here.*

Aella felt sad. Why? Every time she looked at Fox, her heart felt as if it would tear out of her chest. *May I stay in touch with you as I work with this site?* she asked.

Of course. Fox wanted nothing more than to be here with her. To absorb her ephemeral beauty and hear her speak once more.

Aella's spirit lifted. What *was* this strange connection between them? Her curiosity was strong, but she had more pressing matters. In the next few days, Aella knew her life would change forever. How, she had no idea....

Look for REUNION
by USA TODAY *bestselling*
author Lindsay McKenna,
available April 2010, only from
Silhouette® Nocturne™.

2 Stories in 1

HER MEDITERRANEAN PLAYBOY

Sexy and dangerous—he wants you in his bed!

The sky is blue, the azure sea is crashing against the golden sand and the sun is hot.

The conditions are perfect for a scorching Mediterranean seduction from two irresistible untamed playboys!

Indulge your senses with these two delicious stories

A MISTRESS AT THE ITALIAN'S COMMAND
by Melanie Milburne

ITALIAN BOSS, HOUSEKEEPER MISTRESS
by Kate Hewitt

Available April 2010 from Harlequin Presents!

www.eHarlequin.com

HP12910

HARLEQUIN® Romance®

ROMANCE, RIVALRY
AND A FAMILY REUNITED

THE BRIDES *of* BELLA ROSA

William Valentine and his beloved wife, Lucia, live
a beautiful life together, but when his former love Rosa
and the secret family they had together resurface,
an instant rivalry is formed. Can these families
get through the past and come together as one?

Step into the world of Bella Rosa
beginning this April with

Beauty and the Reclusive Prince
by

RAYE MORGAN

Eight volumes to collect and treasure!

www.eHarlequin.com

HR17650

HARLEQUIN®

INTRIGUE®

WILL THIS REUNITED FAMILY
BE STRONG ENOUGH TO EXPOSE
A LURKING KILLER?

FIND OUT IN THIS ALL-NEW
THRILLING TRILOGY FROM TOP
HARLEQUIN INTRIGUE AUTHOR

B.J. DANIELS

WHITEHORSE
MONTANA

Winchester Ranch

GUN-SHY BRIDE—*April 2010*

HITCHED—*May 2010*

TWELVE-GAUGE GUARDIAN—
June 2010

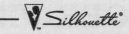

SPECIAL EDITION

INTRODUCING A BRAND-NEW MINISERIES FROM *USA TODAY* BESTSELLING AUTHOR

KASEY MICHAELS

SECOND-CHANCE BRIDAL

At twenty-eight, widowed single mother Elizabeth Carstairs thinks she's left love behind forever....until she meets Will Hollingsbrook. Her sons' new baseball coach is the handsomest man she's ever seen—and the more time they spend together, the more undeniable the connection between them. But can Elizabeth leave the past behind and open her heart to a second chance at love?

FIND OUT IN

SUDDENLY A BRIDE

*Available in April
wherever books are sold.*

LARGER-PRINT
BOOKS!

 **HARLEQUIN** *Presents*

PASSION
GUARANTEED
SEDUCTION

GET 2 FREE LARGER-PRINT
NOVELS PLUS 2 FREE GIFTS!

YES! Please send me 2 FREE LARGER-PRINT Harlequin Presents® novels and my 2 FREE gifts (gifts are worth about $10). After receiving them, if I don't wish to receive any more books, I can return the shipping statement marked "cancel". If I don't cancel, I will receive 6 brand-new novels every month and be billed just $4.55 per book in the U.S. or $5.24 per book in Canada. That's a saving of 13% off the cover price! It's quite a bargain! Shipping and handling is just 50¢ per book in the U.S. and 75¢ per book in Canada.* I understand that accepting the 2 free books and gifts places me under no obligation to buy anything. I can always return a shipment and cancel at any time. Even if I never buy another book, the two free books and gifts are mine to keep forever.

176 HDN E4GC   376 HDN E4GN

Name	(PLEASE PRINT)	
Address		Apt. #
City	State/Prov.	Zip/Postal Code

Signature (if under 18, a parent or guardian must sign)

Mail to the **Harlequin Reader Service:**
IN U.S.A.: P.O. Box 1867, Buffalo, NY 14240-1867
IN CANADA: P.O. Box 609, Fort Erie, Ontario L2A 5X3

Not valid for current subscribers to Harlequin Presents Larger-Print books.

Are you a subscriber to Harlequin Presents books
and want to receive the larger-print edition?
Call 1-800-873-8635 today!

* Terms and prices subject to change without notice. Prices do not include applicable taxes. Sales tax applicable in N.Y. Canadian residents will be charged applicable provincial taxes and GST. Offer not valid in Quebec. This offer is limited to one order per household. All orders subject to approval. Credit or debit balances in a customer's account(s) may be offset by any other outstanding balance owed by or to the customer. Please allow 4 to 6 weeks for delivery. Offer available while quantities last.

Your Privacy: Harlequin Books is committed to protecting your privacy. Our Privacy Policy is available online at www.eHarlequin.com or upon request from the Reader Service. From time to time we make our lists of customers available to reputable third parties who may have a product or service of interest to you. If you would prefer we not share your name and address, please check here. ☐

Help us get it right—We strive for accurate, respectful and relevant communications. To clarify or modify your communication preferences, visit us at www.ReaderService.com/consumerschoice.

HPLP10

HARLEQUIN *Presents*

EXTRA

**Presents Extra brings you
two new exciting collections!**

REGALLY WED
For the prince's bed

Rich, Ruthless and Secretly Royal #97
by ROBYN DONALD

Forgotten Mistress, Secret Love-Child #98
by ANNIE WEST

RUTHLESS TYCOONS
Powerful, merciless and in control!

Taken by the Pirate Tycoon #99
by DAPHNE CLAIR

Italian Marriage: In Name Only #100
by KATHRYN ROSS

*Available April 2010
from Harlequin Presents EXTRA!*